W9-BES-705

of Special Importance to our American Readers

The Case of the 24 MISSING TITLES ...

Over the years many of our American readers have been distressed that Harlequin Romances were published in Canada three months ahead of the United States release date.

We are pleased to announce that effective April 1972 Harlequin Romances will have simultaneous publication of new titles throughout North America.

To solve the problem of the 24 MISSING TITLES (No. 1553 to No. 1576) arrangements will be made with many Harlequin Romance retailers to have these missing titles available to you before the end of 1972.

Watch for your retailer's special display!

If, however, you have difficulty obtaining any of the missing titles, please write us.

Yours truly,

The Publisher
HARLEQUIN ROMANCES.

WELCOME

TO THE WONDERFUL WORLD

of Harlequin Romances!

Interesting, informative and entertaining,
each Harlequin Romance portrays an appealing
love story. Harlequin Romances take you
to faraway places — places with real people
facing real love situations — and
you become part of their story.

As publishers of Harlequin Romances, we're extremely
proud of our books (we've been publishing
them since 1954). We're proud also that Harlequin
Romances are North America's most-read
paperback romances.

Eight new titles are released every month and are
sold at nearly all book-selling stores across
Canada and the United States.

A free catalogue listing all available Harlequin Romances
can be yours by writing to the

HARLEQUIN READER SERVICE,
M.P.O. Box 707, Niagara Falls, N.Y. 14302.
Canadian address: Stratford, Ontario, Canada.

or use order coupon at back of book.

We sincerely hope you enjoy reading
this Harlequin Romance.

Yours truly,

THE PUBLISHERS
Harlequin Romances

THE
LEAPING FLAME

by

BARBARA CUST

HARLEQUIN BOOKS   TORONTO
WINNIPEG

Original hard cover edition published in 1972
by Mills & Boon Limited, 17 - 19 Foley Street,
London W1A 1DR, England

© Barbara Cust 1972

Harlequin edition published May, 1972

SBN 373-01588-7

Printed in Canada

1588

CHAPTER ONE

THE Band of the Royal Marines broke into the strains of "A Life on the Ocean Wave" and the gap between the quayside and the S.S. *Andromeda* widened. Drina Tonbridge, leaning over the ship's rail, gave a gasp of mingled pleasure and excitement at the thought that her holiday had really begun. Somehow she had never been able to believe that she would actually sail away for thirteen days of sun and sea air, but here she was with the deck beneath her and the shores of England receding into the distance.

Everything had happened so quickly, spurred on by the bitter disappointment of receiving Lois's letter. All those months of saving hard and of taking temporary jobs because the pay was higher than for permanent work and there was no having to give a month's notice if you wanted to leave suddenly, and then her dream being shattered by those few scrawled words—"I'm afraid things haven't worked out very well. The truth is that Steven can't find an hotel site at the price he wants to pay, so the whole idea looks like being abandoned. We shall probably move on somewhere else, which means that at the moment there's no point in your coming out to join us. I'll write again when we've made fresh plans."

Now that the ship was out in the Channel a chill breeze was springing up, and Drina decided to go down to her cabin and see whether her luggage had arrived. She wheeled abruptly, right into the path of a man who was pausing to look back at the shore, and had to stop short to avoid colliding with him.

"I'm sorry," she apologized, and he smiled, a charming smile which made her realize how handsome he must have been as a young man, though now his thick hair was white and his shoulders were slightly bowed.

"No harm done," he answered. "It's a wonderful feeling, isn't it, to know that for a short while we can leave all our worries behind? That's the beauty of a cruise. You can be as gregarious as you wish, or find a quiet corner of the deck and never speak to a soul."

Drina smiled back. "I've never been on a cruise before. I booked on impulse, and then this morning I wondered whether I'd regret it since I'm travelling by myself."

"I'm sure you won't, not unless all the young men on board are blind. Let's take a walk round the deck, shall we? Are you the first or second sitting for lunch?"

"Second sitting," responded Drina.

"So are we; perhaps we'll find ourselves at the same table. My name is Carlyon, Robert Carlyon."

"And I'm Drina Tonbridge."

A deep voice behind them said: "It's far too cold for you to be out here without a coat, Grandfather, and after the journey down I think you ought to rest before lunch."

For the second time, Drina turned abruptly. A tall, dark man stood there, a man whose handsome features proclaimed him to be a relative of her companion, but there the resemblance ended. Instead of the older man's shrewd grey eyes twinkling in a network of wrinkles, the newcomer's were the chilliest Drina had ever seen, as cold as a winter sea, and above them, black brows met in a scowl. The glance he gave her was completely indifferent, and she found herself flushing under his hard stare.

"I'm not a child," said his grandfather irritably, "and a short stroll won't hurt me."

"You were up early this morning, and there's no sense in overdoing things."

"Oh, very well." The older man capitulated suddenly. "We'll meet again, Miss Tonbridge. This is my grandson. Scott, this is Miss Drina Tonbridge."

Scott Carlyon made the merest gesture of acknowledgement and laid his hand firmly on his grandfather's arm while Drina made a dive for the nearest companionway. No one had ever shown her so plainly before that her presence wasn't welcome, and she was smarting with indignation. She hadn't been the one to start the conversation, and that angry young man needn't think she had the slightest desire to pursue his acquaintance. On the contrary, she hoped fervently that she wouldn't come across him again, and since there were almost a thousand passengers on board, she'd be unlucky if she did.

She went down to her cabin on B deck, and finding that her suitcase had arrived, began to unpack. She had paid extra to have an outside double cabin with shower and toilet to herself, and as she admired its compactness and hung her dresses in the wardrobe, she went over once more in her mind the events which had led to her embarking on this voyage to the sun.

Her mother had died when Drina and her twin sister Lois were babies, and her father had brought them up with the aid of a housekeeper until his own death five years ago. The twins were sixteen then, and had, rather reluctantly, been offered a home by their father's sister and her husband. But as soon as they were capable of earning a living, they had struck out on their own and managed to find a tiny flat in London to share. They weren't identical twins, but superficially they were alike, with blonde hair and hazel eyes, though when Lois took up modelling she soon bleached her hair to a silvery fairness which Drina didn't bother to emulate. Lois had the more regular features too, and the longer legs, but Drina's figure was slim and attractive and her smile had a warmth which endeared her to people.

Lois was all set to make her mark in the modelling world, but somehow it didn't quite come off. She managed to keep going with photographic work and the odd television commercial, but it wasn't exactly a life of luxury, and when she met Marc Chelmsford, an art student, she announced blithely that he was the man for her and threw her career to the winds. They married in haste and set off for Ibiza where Marc had been offered a commission to paint murals in the restaurant which a friend of his was opening. Life in the sun appealed to both of them, and Marc was confident that he could earn enough by painting to provide food and a roof over their heads. He scoffed at the idea of a nine-to-five job, and teased Drina about her conventionality when she retorted that they couldn't all be nomads and that personally she preferred three solid meals a day to a crust of bread and a handful of grapes.

She herself had taken a course in shorthand and typing and found a job in a surveyor's office. She took pride in turning out fast and accurate work, and when she was eventually refused a rise, she had no difficulty in obtaining a better paid post.

When Lois went to Ibiza, her place in the flat was taken by Sally Hurdlow who worked in the same office as Drina. At first, Lois's letters were ecstatic about the place and the friends they were making. She loved the life, and she was acting as hostess in the restaurant which was beginning to attract the tourists. The man who owned it was thinking of expanding by opening a small hotel nearby with main meals to be taken in the restaurant, and as he would need extra staff to run it, Lois wondered if Drina would consider coming out to join them. She could cope with the booking of accommodation, deal with correspondence, order supplies and so on. It was just a question of finding a suitable plot of land on which to build, and Steven was confident that that would be quite simple. If building started soon, Drina could come out in the spring to prepare for the summer rush of tourists.

Drina liked the idea and began to take temporary jobs, saving hard all winter so that she would have a little capital to take with her. She didn't arrange any summer holiday because she expected to be in Ibiza by then, but when the middle of July arrived and Lois was still writing evasively that things had been delayed, Drina demanded to know exactly what the situation was.

When she read her sister's reply to her letter she said ruefully to Sally: "I should have known what would happen. Right from the beginning it all sounded too good to be true."

Sally wrinkled her brow. "What a shame! Why

don't you pop over to Ibiza for a holiday and talk to Lois and Marc? You could do with a break, and your present job finishes in a few days."

"Obviously Lois doesn't want me out there or she would have suggested my making the trip. Besides, from what she says in her letter, they will have moved on by now. No, I'll have to wait until she sends me a new address, and in the meantime I'll take a short holiday in England."

But, passing a travel agency, the advertisment for sunshine cruises caught her eye, and on an impulse she went in. Half an hour later she had recklessly booked a double cabin for herself, and the greater part of the money she had saved had been signed away. There had been a cancellation on a cruise sailing in the first week of August, and she had been overcome by the longing to see the ports featured on it—Madeira, Gibraltar, Palma and Lisbon. She would at least have some sunshine to console her for another winter spent in England.

And now here she was at sea at last, and looking forward to every minute of the thirteen days afloat. She hoped it wouldn't be rough in the Bay of Biscay, but that was something she would have to risk. She had crossed the Channel once on a cheap holiday to Paris, but it had been in a flat calm so she didn't know what kind of sailor she was. Well, now was her chance to find out.

A card on her dressing table informed her that she was on the second sitting for meals, and the steward knocked to tell her that second lunch would be served at half past one, and to ask what time she would like her morning tea. She decided to have it at eight, since breakfast was at nine, and then she went in search of the restaurant which was on D

Deck, two decks below. The first sitting of lunch was just over, and she consulted the plan at the entrance to the restaurant to find out the position of her table.

It lay to the left of the room, and as she made her way towards it she saw that she was the first arrival. Almost immediately she was joined by two middle-aged spinster sisters who introduced themselves as Hester and Janet Fleming, and a married couple named Fanshawe, then a dark man came along and gave his name as Don Madderley. His manner was friendly to them all, but Drina was aware that he eyed her more appreciatively than the Misses Fleming.

"Drina," he commented. "That's an unusual name. I don't think I've come across it before."

"It's short for Alexandrina," confessed Drina. "I was called after my grandmother, but I don't even remember her."

"And she was probably called after Queen Victoria," said Janet Fleming pedantically, "whose full name was Alexandrina Victoria. In fact, I think I recall reading that she was known as Drina when she was a little girl."

Don Madderley gave Drina such a droll look that she couldn't help smiling warmly at him, and at that moment the last two occupants of the table arrived and sat down. Drina's smile vanished abruptly. Oh no, it wasn't possible that fate had played such a miserable trick on her as to put her at the same table as Robert Carlyon and his grandson.

But there they were, seating themselves opposite the Misses Fleming. As Robert Carlyon unfolded his napkin he caught sight of Drina, and beamed at her.

"So we meet again?"

"Yes," agreed Drina, trying to look pleased but

conscious all the time of Scott Carlyon's impassive features at the other side of the table. Mealtimes weren't going to be exactly cheerful occasions if she had to face him three times a day.

He roused himself, however, to answer Hester Fleming politely when she made a remark while his grandfather chatted affably, revealing that he had come on the cruise to recuperate from an illness. Don Madderley made general conversation too, but towards the end of the meal he said casually to Drina: "What do you intend to do this afternoon? Find a sheltered corner to be lazy in, or will you take me on at deck quoits?"

"Well, first I'd like to explore the ship and get my bearings."

"Fine, we'll do it together. I've a rough idea of the layout, and there's a direction board on each deck."

It didn't take them long to discover the library, the swimming pool, the cinema, and the five different bars the ship boasted. Then they strolled round the promenade deck several times so that Drina's cheeks were glowing as they went down to the restaurant for tea.

The two Miss Flemings were there, but Don took Drina's elbow and steered her towards another table.

"We shall see quite enough of them at regular mealtimes," he said, "along with the others. The old boy's quite a cheerful soul, but the grandson isn't very forthcoming."

"Carlyon isn't a usual name," remarked Drina, "but I've heard it before, only I can't place the connection."

"Perhaps it was a firm your employer had dealings with?"

"No, but it did crop up at one of the places where I've worked."

"Don't rack your brains and it will come to you suddenly. Do you want a cake? Then shall we go up on deck again?"

Drina rose, and he pulled a chair out of her way so that she could pass.

"I suppose they make these chairs heavy so that they'll stay anchored when the ship rolls," he said, and Drina gave an exclamation.

"Of course! Scott Carlyon, he's the man who designed the award-winning chair. You must have heard of him."

Don looked blank. "Sorry, his name doesn't ring a bell with me."

"I had a temporary job last autumn as secretay to the managing director of a big oil combine, and the boardroom there had been furnished by Carlyons. I must admit it looked good. The table was made out of segments of differently grained woods, and the whole effect was magnificent."

"Do you know a lot about furniture?"

"Very little really, but this man I worked for was interested in it, and keen on the hand-made pieces which Carlyons specialize in."

"Mm, sounds very nice. I must mention them to my own firm. Now, what shall we do this evening— dance in the ballroom or play darts in the Little Brown Jug?"

In the end they settled for dancing, but Drina decided to have an early night since she was suddenly feeling tired. The ship was rolling slightly, but once she was in her bunk the motion lulled her off to sleep, and she didn't wake until the next morning when a patch of sunlight on the ceiling above her porthole told her that it was a fine day. At eight the steward knocked with early morning tea and the daily news sheet, so as she sipped she was able to contemplate the day's programme.

There was certainly plenty of entertainment offered—dancing, a cinema show, deck games, lectures, light music, and a quiz. As it was Sunday there was Divine Service conducted by the captain in the ballroom in the morning, and a cricket match on the boat deck in the afternoon. There was the pool if you wanted to swim, or a deck chair if you felt inclined to be lazy; Drina was almost bewildered by the choice offered.

But by the time the ship was through the Bay of Biscay and headed for Madeira, she felt as if she had been at sea all her life. She'd taken her daily constitutional round the deck, played deck quoits and shuffleboard, swum in the pool, bought postcards in the shop and written them so that they could be posted in Madeira, listened to the pop group in the Little Brown Jug, jived in the discothèque, and danced in the ballroom. In most of these activities she had been partnered by Don, and she had enjoyed his company very much. He was good-tempered and lively, but rather put out when he discovered that she had booked in England for an excursion in Madeira which was unfortunately full up.

"Why didn't you wait until you came aboard before booking?" he said aggrievedly at dinner the night before, "and then we could have gone somewhere together?"

"Because I was anxious to have a toboggan ride," said Drina. "I've been reading that you're pulled down these steep cobbled slopes by two men with ropes, and I didn't want to miss the experience."

"Quite right," chuckled Robert Carylon. "Never miss the opportunity of trying something new."

"Surely you're not going to take the trip, Mr. Carylon?" said Miss Hester Fleming incredulously.

"No, it's too spine-jarring at my age. Besides, I did it some years ago. I've visited Madeira several times; it's one of my favourite places. I shall take a taxi to a restaurant I know which stands high above a valley, and have a leisurely meal ashore."

"Well, I shall look at the shops in Funchal," decided Miss Hester. "I should like to buy a table-cloth in that beautiful Madeira embroidery, but I expect they'll be rather expensive."

The ship was due to reach Madeira in the early hours of the morning, and Drina resolved to get up early and swim in the pool before breakfast since she would be away from the ship all day. She decided to go along about half past seven so that she could drink her early morning tea when she got back, and it took her only a moment to slip into her bikini and, with a towelling wrap over it, make her way to A Deck.

There were only one or two energetic souls about, and for a moment she thought she might have the pool to herself. Then when she came out of the ladies' changing room where she left her wrap she saw that there was already someone in the pool, a man who appeared to be lying on the bottom. Her heart gave a great leap at the thought that he might be drowning, then he slid forward like a fish and surfaced.

As she stood on the rim staring at him, he shook the wet hair from his eyes and she saw that it was Scott Carlyon. Immediately she felt cheated. She'd made the effort to get up early and now everything was spoilt because he was already in possession.

"Good morning," she forced herself to say, and he

answered: "Good morning," in a cold, uninterested voice, then submerged again.

Her face burning, Drina dived in, but haste made her clumsy and she struck the water with a splash. She was a competent swimmer and she loved the water, but as she paused for breath she had to admit that she wasn't in the same class as Scott Carlyon. He was more like a fish than a human being, and he could swim under water for the whole length of the pool with no visible effort at all.

The temperature of the water was around eighty, which made it sheer bliss to bathe. Drina felt she could have stayed in for hours, but she was having breakfast earlier than usual because of her excursion so, reluctantly, she climbed out of the pool and made for the dressing-room to collect her wrap. When she came out in it Scott Carlyon had gone, for which she was thankful. It was annoying to think that if she wanted an early morning swim she ran the risk of bumping into him every time, but why should she give it up?

She heard the sound of voices as she walked along the deck, and noticed a cluster of people leaning over the side. Joining them, she could see that in the hope of persuading the passengers to buy a flock of small boats had come out from the mainland with a cargo of gay souvenirs.

"Five pounds," called a boatman hopefully, holding up a toy yacht. "Very fine boat, lady. You buy?"

Lines weighted with lead were thrown up to the rails where they were caught and secured. Then a basket containing a doll dressed in local costume, a musical box and a set of mats was hauled up, and a spate of bargaining began. After watching for a few minutes Drina went back to her cabin and began to dress. Not slacks or shorts this morning as she was going ashore, but a crisp white dress banded in navy, and white sling-back sandals.

Seating at the breakfast table was informal this morning, and only the young married couple were already there. Drina ate melon and fresh rolls with honey, then went back to her cabin to pick up her sun-glasses and a scarf. She glanced at her watch. It wasn't as late as she'd thought, barely nine o'clock, and her coach didn't leave until a quarter past.

Making her way to the gangway on C Deck she discovered that the traders had already come aboard, and were spreading out their wares on the deck. The embroidered goods were really beautiful, and she stopped to look at some handkerchiefs and a blouse. She bought the handkerchiefs, but decided that the blouse was too expensive, then looked at her watch again. To her horror she discovered that it still registered nine o'clock which meant that it must have stopped, but when?

As quickly as possible she rushed down the gangway and along the quayside. Round the corner stood a coach, but as she approached she could see it was numbered B, a tour which she remembered didn't depart until half past nine. Even as she watched it lumbered out, and then there were no coaches left at all. Despondently she began to walk slowly back along the quayside. Her coach had evidently gone out on time, and she had missed it. It was her own fault, but that wasn't much consolation.

She reached the foot of the gangway as two figures came down it, and though she turned immediately, it was too late.

"Why," said Robert Carlyon, "what are you doing here? I thought you would be on your way to the mountains by now. Wasn't your coach supposed to leave at quarter past nine?"

"It did," said Drina wryly, "but unfortunately I wasn't on it. My watch had stopped, and by the time I realized it the coach had gone."

"Too bad, and you were so looking forward to your toboggan ride."

"Oh, it doesn't matter," said Drina hastily. "I'll potter about Funchal. I shall enjoy looking at the shops."

"That sounds a tame way to spend the day. I've got a better idea. Join us, and you and Scott can come down by toboggan from Terreiro da Lucta while I stay in the taxi."

"Oh no," stammered Drina in horror, "I'd hate you to change your plans because of me. I shall be quite all right on my own, really I shall."

She wished fervently that she'd never mentioned the toboggan run at the dinner table. She could imagine nothing worse than being alone with Scott Carlyon since he so patently didn't want her company, but Robert Carlyon wasn't to be denied.

"Nonsense," he said with the air of a man who was used to being obeyed. "It won't mean changing our plans at all. We'll make a slight detour after we've had lunch at our restaurant, and everything will be fine. Ah, this looks like our taxi. Get in, Drina."

It was obviously useless to protest any further, so she climbed into the taxi. She was thankful to see that Scott Carlyon took the seat beside the driver, leaving the back for his grandfather and Drina. The old man smiled at her.

"This has turned out very fortunate for us," he said. "It's much better to have a lady's company than for two men to be on their own. You'll enjoy seeing something of Madeira. I first came here several years ago and fell in love with it at once. I've been back a number of times, and the owner of the restaurant where we're going to lunch has tried to persuade me to buy a villa here."

Drina liked Mr. Carlyon and it had been kind of him to invite her to accompany them, but as the taxi turned into one of the main streets of Funchal and she saw the little curtained carriages drawn by oxen which were for hire by tourists wanting a trip through the town, she wished she were alone in one.

Almost immediately the road began to climb, and they passed pretty villas with roofs of red curving tiles until most of these were left behind and they were among the plantations of sugar cane and bananas. Everywhere there were masses of flowers. Walls were covered in bougainvillea, crimson, orange and white; there were scarlet hibiscus, pink oleanders blue and white agapanthus and plantations of orange lily-like flowers called bird of paradise. The scent of the pines and eucalyptus trees was heady in the sun, and the grapes hung in great purple clusters.

"Oh, it's lovely!" breathed Drina, and Robert Carlyon looked pleased.

"We'll stop before long and have some coffee at a place where there's a breathtaking view."

In a short while the taxi halted and they all got out. Robert Carlyon led Drina to a low stone wall, and said : "There, what do you think of that?"

Below them, the ground fell away in a series of terraces to the sea. The water was azure streaked with emerald, and the sun glowed over the whole landscape. Here and there were houses and small stone thatched sheds.

"Those are where the animals live," said Robert Carlyon. "Every scrap of ground is used for cultivation here, so there's no grazing for the stock which has to be kept indoors."

"It's so steep that I can't imagine how they reach some of the terraces," said Drina. "It must be hard work climbing up to them."

"It's hard work all right," said Scott Carlyon dryly. "Up at dawn and to bed at sunset."

He managed to imply that Drina didn't know what work was, and she bit back a sharp retort. She wouldn't spoil the day for the old man by quarrelling with his grandson, but it wasn't easy to swallow her resentment at his attitude.

The tiny restaurant sold coffee, but a car was already parked outside it with a group of tourists buying postcards, so Drina wandered down a path by the side of it to inspect the great leaves of the yams which bordered it. A curious flight of steps with the treads made up of small cobbles led to a garden, and when she stared up at it she saw that freshly washed linen had been spread on the bushes to dry. An old woman was standing on a balcony attached to the upper storey of the house, her face brown and seamed with wrinkles. She was clad all in rusty black, and Drina wondered what she thought of the tourists in their brief, colourful clothes.

There were two tables outside the restaurant, but they were both occupied, so Scott Carlyon carried the coffee to the stone wall where they sat drinking it.

"We're lucky to get the full benefit of the view

today," said Robert Carlyon. "Sometimes the mist comes down in a matter of minutes and blots out everything."

The coffee drunk, they got back into the taxi, and were driven leisurely along the winding roads, past plantations of sugar cane interplanted with runner beans. The grapes were grown in places right over the roofs of the houses, and great banks of blue hydrangeas bordered the roadside. Soon the road ran through a village where the streets were cobbled and a woman led a small black pig on a string.

"I never thought to see that," said Drina, laughing. "Oh, there's a market!"

"Would you like to have a look at it?" asked Robert Carlyon, and in response to his command the driver pulled up obediently.

"I shan't get out of the car, but Scott will walk round with you," said his grandfather, and Drina bit her lip in vexation at having precipitated the very situation she wanted to avoid.

Reluctantly, she got out of the taxi, and walked with Scott Carlyon to the market stalls.

"I'm sorry," she said stiffly. "This must be very boring for you."

His mouth twitched sardonically. "Not at all, there's always something fresh to see. Are you very interested in fruit and vegetables?"

"Yes, I am," retorted Drina defiantly, "when they're strange to me. What's in that basket over there?"

"Custard apples, and that's garlic hanging up above them. These are passion fruit."

"Oh, pomegranates! I haven't seen those for ages. They look so fascinating inside that I feel I ought to enjoy them, but the taste reminds me of rusty tins."

Everything was heaped in profusion, and the local women were examining the goods very carefully before they bought. Drina would have liked to linger, but she didn't want to keep Robert Carlyon waiting, so she walked to the end of the market, then turned back to the taxi. Just as she was about to get in Scott Carlyon touched her arm.

"Look over there at what that man's carrying."

Drina turned her head and saw a man with something on his back entering a doorway. It was almost as if he had an animal on his shoulders, and yet the shape wasn't quite right.

"It's a wineskin," said Scott Carlyon, interpreting her puzzled frown. "They take the skin of a cow or a goat and use it to transport the local wine."

"I've often read of wineskins in books, but somehow I never imagined they left the legs on," said Drina absurdly. "I'd always visualized them as round."

Scott Carlyon laughed. It was the first time she had seen him with a relaxed expression, and it didn't last more than a second. Then he was looking at his watch and saying: "If we want to reach the restaurant in good time for lunch then we oughtn't to linger here."

"No need to hurry," said his grandfather easily, but Drina stepped hastily inside the taxi, feeling guilty.

The restaurant was long and low and stood in a picturesque garden. In the dining-room the walls were painted, and through the heavy beams lacing the ceiling could be seen the underside of the roof tiles. The waitresses were all dressed in national costume which consisted of a gaily striped skirt worn with a white blouse, and a cape which was passed over the left shoulder and then fastened beneath the other arm. On their feet they wore short calfskin boots, and they moved gracefully between the tables, never hurrying but without any delay.

Mr. Carlyon was greeted like an old friend by the proprietor.

"Ah, Senhor Carlyon, it is good to see you again. You will consider buying a villa this time, yes?"

"I'm still thinking about it, Senhor Gonzales," said Robert Carlyon, "and when the winter's cold and wet in England I'm seriously tempted."

"You only have to say the word and my brother-in-law will find the right one for you," Senhor Gonzales assured him. "And now let me show you to your table. It is the one in the corner which you prefer."

Drina enjoyed the meal. It started with a piquant tomato and potato soup, followed by delicious fried fish with croutons, boiled potatoes and a salad of tomato and lettuce. Then came lamb with green and red peppers and tiny fried potato balls, followed by a rich honeycomb sweet and then a basket of fresh fruit—grapes, bananas, plums and green figs. Last of all, the waitress came round with a bowl of passion fruit which was deliciously ice cold and refreshing. With the meal they drank the local wine, and when they had finished Drina felt she could hardly move.

"We'll have our coffee in the garden," said Robert Carlyon, and led the way to the terrace shaded by vine leaves. The sun lay in golden splashes on the table, and sitting back sipping her coffee, Drina felt at peace with the world.

Her host's eyelids drooped, and when he murmured drowsily: "Why don't you go and explore the garden?" she thought it only tactful to agree.

As she got up, Scott Carlyon rose to his feet, and she said hastily: "You stay and finish your coffee. I'm going to stroll under the trees," and she darted off without giving him the chance to follow her.

On the far side of the garden the ground sloped down steeply, and in the distance she could see a line of sea. At the bottom of the valley was the stony bed of a stream, and though there was only a trickle of water in it, a woman was washing, laying the linen on the rocks to bleach and dry in the sun.

A voice behind her said: "No spin-driers here," and she answered soberly: "No. It certainly is a hard life; no wonder the people look old and wrinkled. On the other hand, they have much more tranquil expressions than we have. Those waitresses in the restaurant, I don't suppose they earn a great deal, but their faces were so serene."

"You have a point there. They were gentle and quiet, not greedy and grasping like the majority of women these days."

"That's rather a sweeping statement," countered Drina indignantly. "Lots of Englishwomen are gentle and quiet too."

"Are they?" He raised his eyebrows. "Then I must have been unfortunate in the ones I've met."

"Yes," she agreed baldly, aware that she didn't sound very convincing. Then she went on: "There's no need for you to come down in the toboggan with me. If you can head your grandfather off the idea I'll back you up."

"Thank you," he said smoothly, "but I think it might be simpler to go through with it. You made such a play at the dinner table last night of wanting the experience that I don't think anything you

24

could say now would convince him that you'd changed your mind. Let me congratulate you on the act you put on when you so carefully missed the coach this morning."

"I don't know what you mean!" gasped Drina.

"Oh, I think you do. My grandfather wouldn't have been taken in so easily some years ago, but of course he is seventy-five now."

Drina flushed scarlet, but before she could say anything more Robert Carlyon appeared.

"So there you are! If we push on now we shall have time for tea in Funchal before we go back to the ship. Come along, Drina."

"I've changed my mind," she said desperately. "I don't want to go down by toboggan. I'll return with you in the taxi."

"Nonsense, you will enjoy being bumped over the cobbles."

Back in the taxi Drina seethed with rage. She'd never hated anyone in her life as much as she hated Scott Carlyon. She longed to tell him exactly what she thought of him for his unjustified suspicions, but she didn't want to upset his grandfather. As it was, she was obliged to get out at Terreiro da Lucta and allow herself to be helped into one of the basketwork toboggans which, furnished with cushions and standing on wooden runners, were ready to start the journey over the old cobbled road to Funchal.

Scott took his place beside her and then the sledge started off, guided by two men each holding a controlling rope. The sledge swayed and bounced, gliding round the steep turns in the road at what seemed a terrifying speed. Small children lined the roadside, flinging flowers into Drina's lap, and she tossed all her small change out to them.

They swung round a curve, and as Drina felt herself slide to one side Scott's arm came round her waist, holding her firmly. She jerked herself against it in protest, but he merely said: "Sit still unless you want to be a mass of bruises," so resentfully she subsided. She had never been so conscious of anything in her life as that arm pressing against her like a bar of iron as they sped through the woods down to the streets of Funchal.

CHAPTER TWO

DON was aggrieved when he found that she had spent the day in the company of the Carlyons.

"Why didn't you let me know that you'd missed the coach?" he protested. "We could have gone about together and had a wonderful time."

"Mr. Carlyon didn't really give me the chance to do anything but accept his offer. I couldn't get out of going with them unless I hurt his feelings."

"What about my feelings?"

Drina smiled. "Now confess, you enjoyed yourself very well without me."

"Not half as much as I should have done with you, but I'll forgive you if you'll come up on the Boat Deck tonight. We should have a perfect view of the bay from there."

They did. The air was as warm as milk with only the faintest of breezes, and Madeira, seen from the ship, was like fairyland. A jewelled necklace of lights threaded its way right up the mountains, and the Cathedral in Funchal was floodlit, together with several other prominent buildings. Drina and Don leaned over the rail, looking towards the shore.

He said huskily: "This is like a scene from a film, you know, where the hero and heroine first realize that they've fallen in love with each other."

"And that they'll have to part because he's already married or she's already married or they're both already married," said Drina lightly.

She liked Don and enjoyed his company, but she

certainly wasn't in love with him and she didn't want
him waxing sentimental and spoiling the evening.

"It needn't be like that."

"But it invariably is." All at once Drina heard the
sound of singing, and as she looked down into the
water she saw a gaily illuminated launch come into
sight. On its open deck a party of folk dancers, the
girls dressed like the waitresses Drina had seen in the
restaurant, the men in shirts, breeches and tasselled
caps, were gliding and stamping to the lively music of
a three-piece band. The launch cruised slowly along as
the dancers twirled, their reds and golds making brilliant spots of colour against the dark water.

"Quick!" cried Drina. "Let's go down to A Deck.
We'll get a better view of them there."

She ran down the two companionways, followed by
Don, and joined the throng of people lining the rails.
One gay tune followed another, and then at last the
dancers waved farewell and the launch set out for the
shore.

"That was enchanting," sighed Drina. "What a wonderful night! It seems a pity to go to bed."

"No need for that yet." Don pulled her arm through
his. "Come back to the Boat Deck."

Drina shook her head. "No, Don, it's getting late."

She wasn't in the least tired, but she knew that if she
went back to the Boat Deck he would want to make
love to her, and it wasn't fair to encourage him if she
meant to hold off.

"Then come to the Pool Bar and have a drink."

"Thank you, but I really don't want anything more."

Drina gently disengaged her arm, and stepped from
the deck into the nearest alleyway. Don followed her
sulkily as she walked down the companionway to B
Deck.

"Good night," she said as they reached her cabin door, and then suddenly he had pulled her into his arms and his mouth was crushing hers.

For a moment Drina struggled, and then as she realized it was useless she subsided. It wasn't until she was gasping for breath that Don released her, and then as she swayed slightly, she saw that a man was coming towards them, the last person in the world she wanted to encounter at that moment.

She looked straight into the glacial eyes of Scott Carlyon, and his mouth curled with contempt as he passed them.

Drina said furiously: "You had no right to do that!" Then her anger ebbed as Don said placatingly: "I'm sorry, but I couldn't help myself. I've been wanting to kiss you all evening, but you're so maddeningly elusive. Forgive me?"

"Yes, but I don't like being grabbed."

"I promise not to do it again unless I have your wholehearted co-operation," said Don with mock penitence. "Good night, Drina."

Once inside her cabin she undressed and slid into the lower bunk, but though she turned out the light she couldn't sleep. Scott Carlyon's look of scorn was burned into her memory, and she couldn't wipe out the humiliation she had experienced when he had shown so plainly what he thought of her.

The next morning was devoted to water sports in the pool, and here the undoubted star was Scott. He stayed on the greasy pole longer than anyone else and picked up no fewer than twenty-five spoons from the bottom of the pool. Much as she disliked him, Drina couldn't help admiring the way he slid through the water like a fish, and she joined in the congratulations which were heaped on him at lunch by the others at the table.

"How clever of you to be able to swim like that," said Miss Janet Fleming. "Do you live by the sea?"

"No, in a village in Hampshire," said Scott, "but we're not very far from the coast and I've done a great deal of swimming ever since I was a child."

"Ever thought of having a pool of your own?" enquired Don.

"Several times," answered Scott, "but I've never done anything about it."

"Tell the truth," said his grandfather. "You've never done anything about it because your aunt can't bear to part with her rose garden. It's the only possible place for a pool, but she doesn't want to sacrifice it."

"Why should she?" said Scott shortly. "Anyway, I'm more interested in commissioning a really large pool which could be used by our factory workers and the villagers as well. What I'd like to do is rebuild the Village Hall as a community centre with a swimming pool attached."

"That sounds an attractive scheme," said Don. "What's the available site area?"

"That depends whether we can get the piece of land we're negotiating for," Scott told him. "If we can buy it, as we hope, then the planning stage comes next."

"I'm with a firm of architects and we'd be happy to submit an estimate," said Don. "Here's my card. When you've bought your land, give me a ring and I'll come and inspect your site. Our fees are really competitive. I don't think you'd do better anywhere."

"Thanks." Scott took the card, and the conversation became general.

The next port of call was Gibraltar, and here Don monopolized Drina much to his own satisfaction. The ship had arranged for tours of the Rock by taxi, and Drina duly saw St. Michael's Cave with its wonderful stalagmites and stalactites, stood on the ramparts of the old fortress, and was amused by the antics of the apes in the trees on the Upper Rock. There was one appealing baby whom she tried to coax to take a banana, but even as she held out the fruit a wicked old male with grey whiskers snatched it from her and gobbled it up.

"Oh!" she cried in surprise, and Don chuckled as he lowered his camera.

"Just in time to get that shot," he said. "It should come out well with the blue of the sky, the brown of the rock and the yellow of your dress."

It was one of the most attractive dresses Drina possessed, a sleeveless yellow sheath which enhanced the golden tan she was already acquiring. Don's eyes lingered on her admiringly, and she said quickly: "Let's go down into Main Street, look at the shops and find a cool drink."

They sat out on a small piazza under a striped umbrella, and Drina sighed with pleasure.

"To think that it's probably raining in London while we're basking in the sunshine here!"

"Then you're glad you came?" said Don. He put his hand over hers on the table. "So am I. I've enjoyed this morning so much. You'll let me take you out in Palma, won't you? I've been to Majorca before, and I know a hotel round the curve of the bay with its own private beach where we can have lunch on the terrace."

"It sounds delightful," acknowledged Drina, "but I don't want to think of Palma just yet. The holiday's going quickly enough as it is."

The next night there was a Starlight Ball on deck, the perfect setting for romance with soft music and moonlight turning the ship into a dream world. Drina, dancing with Don, found herself possessed by a queer restlessness. The setting was perfect, Don was good-looking and attentive, but there was something missing. She danced past the edge of the pool, and saw Mr. Carlyon sitting at a table with a drink. He raised his hand in salute and then as the music stopped Don touched her arm and said : "Let's go and look at the water."

With scarcely a pause the band broke into a dreamy waltz, and she shook her head.

"Not for a moment. I'm going to dance with Mr. Carlyon."

She turned back to the old man's table, and said laughingly : "Doesn't this take you back to your youth? Will you dance it with me?"

He rose immediately. "With pleasure."

He danced correctly and rather stiffly, but Drina could see that he was enjoying himself. Then suddenly she became aware that someone was standing in the shadow on the verandah which fringed the pool. She missed a step, and Robert Carlyon said : "Oh dear, my breath's giving out. Scott, I relinquish my pretty partner to you."

Before she could protest he had thrust her into his grandson's arms, and Scott's hard strength was holding her to him as he picked up the beat.

It was indignation, of course, at being handed over like a parcel which caused her to feel so breathless, and then that indignation was intensified as Scott said mockingly : "That was very skilfully done."

"What was?" She wasn't sure what he meant, but she guessed his remark wasn't intended to be complimentary.

"The way you flattered my grandfather's ego by asking him to dance with you. I wonder exactly what your motive was."

"I merely thought it might give him pleasure to dance a waltz."

"I'm sure it did, though I understand he was never much of a dancer even in his youth. It's fascinating to watch you playing up to each other, but you mustn't underestimate him, you know. He usually gets what he wants in the end, so be very sure it will be what you want too."

Drina said slowly: "I don't understand. You talk as if your grandfather's playing some kind of game, and as if I'm involved in it. I can assure you that I'm not."

"Then you don't need to worry, do you?"

The music stopped, and Drina was immediately claimed by Don. She turned back to him in relief, disturbed by Scott's words, though she couldn't imagine what he was talking about. Now they were dancing a cha-cha-cha and she gave herself up to the enjoyment of the rhythm, thrusting any thought of Scott out of her mind, and when the dance was over she was glad to see that he'd disappeared from the deck.

When the ship reached Palma she allowed Don to take her to the hotel he had spoken of, and they had a delightful time bathing, eating and watching a cabaret in the evening.

"Today's been wonderful," he said as they took a taxi back to the ship. "I've never enjoyed a holiday more than this one, Drina."

"Neither have I," she concurred. "I hate to think that it's nearly over."

"But we're not going to lose sight of each other when it is. I'm hopping about the country a good deal, but London's my base."

"I may not be in London this winter," said Drina. "I was supposed to go out to Ibiza to join my sister and brother-in-law, but the plan fell through and left me

33

feeling rather at a loose end. I was contemplating trying for a job out of town."

"What kind of job?"

"Secretarial. That's what I'm trained for."

"My firm's always looking for secretaries," he told her. "I'll make some enquiries when I get back. The head office is in London, but we've a branch in Surrey and one in Sussex where there could be openings."

"Thank you," said Drina, wishing she hadn't spoken. She didn't really want to work for the same firm as Don since it might make for complications later on, but perhaps she needn't worry. Probably once the cruise was over he would forget all about her.

Lisbon was the last port of call, and here Drina decided to have a lazy morning in the city and to visit Cintra in the afternoon. Don, who was anxious to see a stock farm, tried hard to persuade her to go with him, but she was firm.

"I want to prowl round the shops," she told him, "and you wouldn't enjoy that."

She had a leisurely breakfast, then took a taxi from the quay to Black Horse Square and from there walked to the Rua Garrett. Here the clothes were hand-made and really lovely, but most of them were too expensive for her and she had to content herself with buying a white sleeveless blouse delicately embroidered in blue. Feeling hot and thirsty, she walked along the Avenida da Liberdade and sat down at one of the tables under the trees to have a drink, but she hadn't been there more than a moment when a familiar figure walked up and sat down beside her. It was Mr. Carlyon, and Drina stared at him in astonishment.

"I thought you were staying on board this morning," she said.

"So did Scott," he confessed, "but I gave him the

slip. I wanted to be on my own for a while so that I could have the chance of putting a proposition to you."

"But how did you manage to find me? I could have been anywhere."

"Not if you were going to look at the best shops. I've been strolling round this area all morning, and I thought I should come across you sooner or later."

The waiter came up, and Mr. Carlyon ordered two glasses of *vinho verde*.

"You'll find it refreshing after your labours," he said. "What do you think of Lisbon?"

"What I've seen of it, I like very much. I wish I'd time to explore further."

"Yes, you'd enjoy taking a trip across the Salazar Bridge and seeing the south bank of the Tagus. Tell me, Drina, you're between jobs at the moment, aren't you, and living in a flat in London?"

"Yes, with a friend, but she'll be getting married soon."

"What will you do then?"

"I'm undecided. I shall need to look for another job when this cruise is over, and I thought I might try something out of London for a change."

"Would you consider coming to work for me?"

"For you? In your office, you mean?"

"No, in my home. As you know I've been ill, and now I have to take things quietly. My doctor wanted me to retire, but I like to go to the factory in the mornings."

"It's a furniture factory, isn't it?"

"Yes. We turn out good quality machine-made pieces, and we also have a small department which executes hand-made commissioned pieces. Scott's in charge of that, and of design generally. I can't pretend all his work's to my taste, but he's making a name for

35

himself and of course more and more of the management will devolve on him."

"And you're going to carry on with some work at home?"

"To fill in my spare time, I've started to write a history of furniture, and I want someone to act as my secretary, tackle the research for me, drive me to the office and so on. I don't think you'd find it a difficult job, but the hours might be staggered which wouldn't suit everyone. On the other hand, you'd have no living expenses, and I should pay you a fair salary."

He named a sum which was more than fair, it was generous, and Drina was taken aback. She had never dreamed of a proposition like this, and she didn't quite know what to say.

Mr. Carlyon went on : "We live in a pleasant village only five miles from a thriving market town, and you'd have the use of a car. You mentioned you were thinking of taking a job out of London, so I imagine the prospect of country life wouldn't worry you. At home there's myself, my daughter who keeps house for me, and Scott. You'd fit in very nicely."

"May I think it over?" asked Drina. "I hadn't contemplated working for a private employer outside an office."

"Take as long as you like to consider it," said Mr. Carlyon. "The only stipulation I make is that if you do accept the post you agree to stay until the first draft of the book is finished. Now we'd better be looking for a taxi if we're to get back to the ship in time for lunch."

Drina was glad to be among a coach load of strangers that afternoon. She couldn't really concentrate on the beauties of the drive to Cintra with the thought of Mr. Carlyon's offer of a job on her mind. She would have been tempted to accept it if it hadn't been for the prospect of living in the same house as Scott. That was something which didn't appeal to her at all, but it was quite likely they wouldn't come much into contact with each other. If she did take this job, she would be able to save a good proportion of her salary, and at the same time she knew that Sally would be glad of the opportunity to get married and take over the flat.

For a short while, exploring the Moorish Royal Palace with its wonderful tiles and then sipping a cool drink outside the Casino in Estoril, Drina shelved her problem, but she knew she would have to thrash it out that evening. Back on the ship she went up on the Promenade Deck to see the last of Lisbon, and stood leaning on the rail as they glided under the Salazar Bridge. A clipped voice behind her said : "I'd like to have a word with you," and she turned to see Scott Carlyon.

She sensed at once that he was very angry, though he had his temper well under control, but she couldn't imagine why. She said : "Of course," and waited to hear what was the matter.

His first words took her so completely by surprise that she could only gape at him.

"You've played your cards very nicely, haven't you? But this is where you come to a full stop."

"I don't understand you," she stammered.

"Don't bother to keep up that pretence any longer. You know exactly what you've been aiming for and so do I. I admit that you've succeeded, but you're not going to get away with it. You're going to tell my grandfather, politely but definitely, that you can't accept this post he's offered you."

Since that was what she was contemplating it was illogical of Drina to feel so furious at this curt order, but she certainly did. It wasn't often that she lost her temper, but when that occurred she lost it thoroughly.

Now her voice was trembling with rage as she flamed: "Am I indeed! And who are you to give me orders?"

"Someone who spotted you from the first moment as a girl on the make—inveigling my grandfather into conversation and letting drop the fact that you hadn't a job to go back to."

"I didn't," stuttered Drina, "that is, not with any ulterior motive. I'm quite capable of finding my own employment."

"Good, then there's no need for us to argue any longer. You can tell my grandfather that you don't want to work for him, and that will be that."

He turned away as if it were all settled with no more to be said, and Drina's fury boiled up anew. But this time she controlled herself. If Scott Carlyon thought he'd won a victory then he was completely mistaken. She'd cut him down to size even if she had to suffer herself in the process.

She said with limpid sweetness: "I repeat I'm quite capable of finding my own employment, but of course this post your grandfather's offered me is most attractive, and it would suit me very well to live in the country for a few months."

Scott's eyes narrowed. "You mean you intend to accept it?"

"Why not?"

"Why, you—" he began dangerously, and then broke off as another voice said: "Here you are, the pair of you. Have you been considering my proposition, Drina?"

This was it. She had either to back down and allow Scott to believe that he'd won, or embroil herself in a situation which would be tricky to say the least. Conscious of those hard eyes on her, Drina's pride rose up. She took a deep breath.

"Yes, I have. I'd like to accept it, and I agree to stay until the first draft of the book is complete."

"Splendid. Can you come straight back with us when the ship docks, or would you prefer a couple of days in London first?"

"It would be more convenient for me to go back to the flat and pick up some clothes, also there'd be arrangements to make with Sally," said Drina, already repenting her hasty decision. She might have triumphed over Scott at the moment, but it was a hollow victory. Now she would have to put up with the consequences of her defiance, and living in the same house he could make things very unpleasant for her.

She'd rather expected him to show his resentment at meals during the last few days of the cruise, but he didn't. He treated her exactly the same as before, and curiously enough this enhanced her fears rather than lulled them. She had an uncomfortable suspicion that he was merely biding his time.

Don was also put out at her decision to work in Hampshire.

"Why do you want to go there?" he grumbled. "We could have seen much more of each other if you'd still been living in London."

"I wanted a change," said Drina. "I'm rather tired of living in that cramped flat. Besides, this job will give me the opportunity to save some money. I'm taken with the idea of getting a job abroad, but I'd like a little capital behind me first."

"Oh well, I suppose Hampshire's reasonably accessible," admitted Don. He brightened. "And if my firm gets the contract to design this community centre Carlyon was talking about I might see quite a lot of you. One thing I'm certain about—I don't intend to allow you to fade out of my life."

Drina smiled, but didn't say anything. She was sure Don meant it at that moment, but hadn't a lot of faith in his constancy. There were a good many attractive girls in the world, and he struck her as being rather susceptible.

They docked at Southampton in the middle of the morning, and disembarked after lunch in groups according to the colour of their landing cards. Drina, who was catching the boat train, went off before either the Carlyons who were driving to Lindisthorpe or Don who was spending the night in Southampton with friends, and arrived at Waterloo in the early evening, taking the Tube from there to Victoria where her flat was situated. Sally was at home to welcome her with a supper of grilled lamb cutlets and tomatoes, and Drina settled down to describe the cruise and hear Sally's news in return.

When she mentioned the Carlyons, and the fact that she'd accepted Robert Carlyon's offer of a job, Sally's eyes rounded.

"But couldn't that be rather dangerous? After all, you don't know anything about them."

"Well, I don't think I'll actually be murdered in my bed," answered Drina airily, "though Scott would dearly like to throttle me. He doesn't approve of me at all."

"Then why——?"

"I shan't be working for him but for his grandfather, and you needn't worry. They're a well-known firm of furniture designers."

"It sounds queer to me," said Sally dubiously. "I thought you were going out to Ibiza to live with Lois and Marc. I know you can't do that at the moment, but when they're settled in a fresh place...."

"*When*," emphasized Drina wryly. "There's no guarantee they'll stay there; they may come back to England. If they don't, I can still go out to them in a few months. This is only a temporary job."

"Well, if you're sure it's all right. I'll admit Andy and I will be glad to rent this flat for a few months. We haven't found anywhere else to live yet, and we were beginning to think we'd have to put off the wedding."

Three days later Drina travelled down to Hampshire, and was met at Canterbridge station by a tall, rather gaunt woman who introduced herself as Elfrida Carlyon.

"My father asked me to come and meet you. Since his illness he rests in the afternoons on doctor's orders, but I expect you know that."

She spoke in a nervous jerky manner, and Drina thought what a pity it was that her tweeds were an ugly snuff colour which did nothing at all for her pale complexion and greying hair. A car was waiting in the station yard, and a man came forward to take Drina's cases from the porter.

"Were you wanting me to stop in the town to pick up anything, Miss Carlyon?" he enquired, and she answered: "No, drive straight home, Hicks, and then you can go back to the factory."

Canterbridge seemed to be a thriving market town, and the road they took out of it passed through a new housing development. Then gradually it gave way to farmland, and before long they came to a tall building well shielded from the road by trees.

"That's the factory," said Elfrida Carlyon. "It was built there so that it could give employment to the people from Lindisthorpe first."

Half a mile further on they reached the village

41

proper. There was a Norman church at one end of the High Street, then a straggle of cottages, and an inn, The Three Feathers. Next came the doctor's Georgian house, with an oval fanlight and a flight of steps, then several shops and a supermarket while the street came to an end with another group of cottages and a square brick building which Drina supposed was the Village Hall. Beyond this came a sharp turning to the right which Hicks took, and a few yards further along was a gate which stood open.

The car swerved inside the gate and up a gravel drive. "Here we are," said Elfrida Carlyon, unnecessarily, and Drina stared up at the house which was to be her home for the next few months.

It was mid-Victorian, but virginia creeper had mellowed the plum-coloured brick, and the windows were long and wide. Through an archway to the left Drina could see what she took to be a stable block, and lawns bordered with shrubs curved away into the distance.

Hicks carried her cases inside and then disappeared. Miss Carlyon led the way up the oak staircase to a large bedroom which overlooked the rose garden at the back of the house.

"I hope you'll be comfortable here," she said. "This room hasn't its own bathroom, but there's one at the end of the passage. Come down when you've unpacked, and we'll have tea. I expect my father will be ready to see you by then."

There was plenty of space for Drina's clothes in the fitted wardrobe which lined one wall of the room. The rest of the furniture was simple in design but very pleasing, and she imagined that the pieces represented some of Carlyons' earliest work. She found the bathroom and washed her hands, then went down to the hall to look about her uncertainly. A door to the right stood ajar so she peeped inside, discovering it to be a drawing-room full of antique pieces in rosewood and mahogany, with long curtains of dull yellow silk at the windows and a beautiful Chinese carpet in blues and yellows on the floor.

"Oh, there you are," said Elfrida Carlyon behind her. "We don't use this room much now, only on special occasions."

"It's very beautiful," said Drina.

"When my sister-in-law, Scott's mother, was here we did a lot of entertaining and gave dinner-parties, but there's been no one to bother since."

"She's dead?" ventured Drina.

"Yes," said Elfrida, one hand plucking nervously at her sweater, then she added quickly: "We'll have tea in the sitting-room."

This was a much smaller room, looking out over the side of the house, with chairs covered in a rose-patterned chintz, and pink curtains.

"I'll just see if Father would like his tea in his room," said Elfrida, but at that moment Robert Carlyon appeared.

"How are you, Drina?" he said with a welcoming smile. "It's good to see you again. Did you have a comfortable journey? I should have liked to come to the station myself to meet you, but that tyrant of a doctor makes me rest every afternoon. No need for it, but it's easier not to argue."

"You're looking very well," Drina told him.

"So are you."

"Tea and a scone, Father?" asked his daughter, holding out a cup and a plate.

"I'll have a cup of tea, but I don't want anything to eat. You know I rarely do in an afternoon."

He spoke irritably, and Drina saw Elfrida Carlyon flush. Her father drained his cup, held it out to be refilled, and said : "What do you think of the house?"

"I like it," answered Drina.

"It lacks the elegance of a Georgian house, but it's solid and well-built and I suppose I'm fond of it because I grew up here. Come along and I'll show you the garden."

He led the way outside, past the rose beds and a long herbaceous border to a kitchen garden set out with vegetable plots and fruit trees. Beyond the kitchen garden was a field screened by a high hedge, and Robert Carlyon said : "That's where Scott hopes to build the Community Centre. He plans to plant a belt of trees between it and this garden to protect our privacy, and the Centre from the prevailing winds."

"It looks an ideal site," commented Drina.

"I'd prefer it to be nearer the factory, but there's no available land there."

"Is your grandson down at the factory this afternoon?"

"Yes, he'll be there until six. Now that I only go in the mornings he has most of the responsibility, but he thrives on it. Just as well since he'll inherit it all eventually. There's no one else to take it over."

Suddenly he seemed to lose interest in the subject, and in Drina herself, because he led the way back to the house, and as soon as they reached the sitting-room he disappeared with a wave of his hand. There was no sign of Miss Carlyon either, and, wondering what she was supposed to do, Drina tentatively explored a passage which she thought might lead to the kitchen quarters. She was right. At the end of it a door stood open, and there was Elfrida Carlyon at a sink washing up the tea things.

44

"Oh." She looked confused when she saw Drina, but the girl went forward and picked up a tea towel lying on a chair.

"Shall I dry for you, Miss Carlyon?"

"Please call me Elfrida since you're going to be one of the family; the other sounds so stiff. I know it's stupid of me not to use the dishwasher, but I'm no good with anything mechanical. I never seem to load it properly, then Mrs. Braine gets cross. I don't want to upset her because it's so difficult to keep a cook here."

"A house this size can't be easy to run."

"It isn't. It's all very well for Father to say that it's solid and well-built, but it also takes a lot of cleaning and girls aren't prepared to do that these days. Sometimes I long for a small modern bungalow or a flat of my own." She paused guiltily. "I shouldn't say that when I've got a comfortable home, but I hate housekeeping and I'm no good at it."

"The garden's very attractive, especially the roses, They must look really beautiful in the summer."

"Are you fond of flowers too?" asked Elfrida eagerly. "I think I get more pleasure out of them than anything else."

"Did you do that arrangement in the hall? I noticed it immediately I entered the house; all those lovely pinks and mauves and purples."

"It's only a hobby," said Elfrida deprecatingly. "I buy all the books I can find on flower arranging, and I enjoy experimenting. I have my own patch where I grow the plants I need for foliage. The pensioner who comes in to look after the garden calls them weeds."

The washing up being finished and the kitchen tidy Elfrida said: "Shall we go out into the garden again and I can show you my favourite spots?"

She led the way, and they cut across the lawns at the

45

front of the house. As they were doing so a yellow sports car went past very fast, and Elfrida said : "I wonder if that's Vanessa's car, but I don't think she's settled in yet."

"Who is Vanessa?" enquired Drina.

"She's the girl Scott was once engaged to. Her people lived at the other side of the village, but she went to Italy and eventually married an Italian who died a few months ago. Now she's coming back to the village."

Elfrida stopped abruptly as if she regretted what she had said, and then began to talk rapidly of something else. Drina felt a faint curiosity about the girl to whom Scott had been engaged. Had she broken it off? If so, Drina couldn't blame her. Scott Carlyon was the very last man she'd choose to marry herself.

CHAPTER THREE

THERE was no mention of Vanessa at the dinner table that evening, in fact, there wasn't much conversation at all. Scott greeted Drina coolly, and she wondered uneasily if it were to be war between them during the whole of her stay at Broomyates. Elfrida was practically dumb, and Robert Carlyon seemed more abstracted than usual. However, when the pudding arrived he took one mouthful, grimaced and dropped his spoon on to his plate.

"This woman's knowledge of cooking's absolutely elementary, Elfrida," he said. "Can't you find someone better?"

His daughter looked unhappy. "I can't, Father. I have tried, but no one wants to come out here and cook unless you're willing to pay really fabulous wages."

Robert Carlyon snorted. "Why should I do that? The salary she's getting is a fair one, and I don't see why I should have to bribe her to turn out anything edible. What we want is someone to run the house properly."

Elfrida flushed. "A living-in housekeeper's worse to find than a cook."

"So it seems. Well, I'm going to the study to look out some notes for the book. Perhaps you'll bring my coffee there."

"Do you want me to come and help?" asked Drina.

"No, certainly not. Plenty of time for you to start tomorrow."

"But if you'll be at the factory in the morning then I'll need some work to carry on with."

"Very well then, perhaps you'll bring my coffee into the study when it's ready and I'll explain what I want you to do."

When the coffee arrived Drina picked up the small tray holding Mr. Carlyon's cup and saucer, and took it to the study. Her employer was sitting at a beautiful rosewood desk with a dark green leather top, there were matching rosewood bookcases on two sides of the room and a handsome mahogany secretaire inlaid with marquetry on the third.

"Come and sit down," he said. "This is where you'll work, and all my reference books are in that bookcase. What I'm hoping to write is not an autobiography but a history of furniture from the earliest times. I made a start on it some months ago, but I haven't got very far. As I'm no typist, all my notes are handwritten, so I think the first thing for you to do is type them, then I can begin to fit them together."

Looking at them, Drina managed to conceal her dismay. Mr. Carlyon's handwriting was very individual and almost indecipherable so that it wasn't going to be at all easy to interpret it. However, he was paying her well for her services so she couldn't expect there to be no snags.

"What a handsome desk," she remarked. "It seems almost a shame to use it."

"Nonsense, it's no good having beautiful things around you if you aren't going to make them part of your life. That bureau, for instance, is French Empire, but I use it to keep my papers in. A lovely old piece of furniture ought to be treated with reverence but not taken out of use. What did you think of the drawing-room?"

"Very handsome but rather formal."

"Which proves my point, because the room's never been used. It needs a woman's touch to bring it to life, but Elfrida has no talent as a hostess."

"You'll have to wait until your grandson marries."

It was meant as a harmless remark, but Robert Carlyon's glance sharpened, and Drina felt suddenly uncomfortable. Perhaps her employer noticed it because he said: "Now that we have a chance to talk, tell me about yourself."

"There's very little to tell. My parents are both dead, and last year my sister married and went to live in Ibiza. She suggested that I should fly out and join her and her husband there, but just as I'd saved enough money to go they decided to move on. I'm not sure exactly where they are at the moment. I haven't heard from Lois since I returned from the cruise."

"I remember your mentioning a sister once. Are there only the two of you?"

"Yes. We're twins, but not identical. Superficially we're alike, but Lois is fairer than I am, and side by side anyone could tell us apart."

"And have you different temperaments?"

"Yes, I think so," answered Drina slowly. "Lois is more impulsive than I am. I'm more cautious."

Robert Carlyon's eyes twinkled. "As when you decided at a moment's notice to work for a stranger?"

Drina flushed, remembering what had really prompted her to accept his offer.

"In this case I felt justified in taking the risk."

"I'm flattered. Well, that's all for tonight. Tomorrow morning you can drive me to the factory after breakfast and then come back and make a start on these notes."

Drina said good night, and went back to the sitting-room. Scott had vanished, but Elfrida was there, half dozing in a chair, and feeling suddenly tired herself, Drina decided to have an early night. She went up to her room and opened the window wide, leaning out to take deep breaths of cool air. Was she going to regret having come to Broomyates? She wasn't sure, but at least if she was unhappy she needn't stay more than a few months.

She came downstairs at eight the next morning, and found Scott and Elfrida already in the dining-room. Scott was finishing his breakfast, but his aunt had barely started hers.

"Good morning, Drina," she said. "What will you have? There's bacon, or a boiled egg if you'd prefer it."

"Only grapefruit and toast, please."

Scott swallowed his last mouthful, and jumped to his feet.

"You're not going to the factory yet, are you?" enquired his aunt.

"Yes. My car's playing up, and I want Hicks to have a look at it."

He went out, and Elfrida sighed.

"If only Scott could meet a nice girl and marry her! It would be lovely to have children in the house again, but of course...." Her voice trailed off, and she rose hurriedly from the table. "I'll get some more hot water and remind Mrs. Braine that Father will soon be down. He doesn't like to be kept waiting for his food."

Drina helped herself to honey. She was curious to see the girl who had once been engaged to Scott Carlyon. Would she be visiting the house or wouldn't she be welcome there?

As it happened she was to see Vanessa sooner than she had anticipated. Whatever Hicks did to Scott's car it proved to be only partially successful because it gave trouble again the next day and had to be left at a garage in Canterbridge for an overhaul. It was to be ready on Saturday, so Robert Carlyon said: "Drina will drive you in to pick it up. She's collecting some reference books I ordered from Smith's."

They drove in after breakfast, Drina praying that she wouldn't do anything foolish because she felt nervous under Scott's critical eye.

He said: "Now that you've been here a week how are you enjoying life at Broomyates?"

"Very much," she answered quickly. "Before I met her I was afraid that your aunt might resent me, but she's made me feel at home."

"Yes, she's a good-natured creature. It's a thousand pities that she didn't marry and have a home of her own. She's far too much under my grandfather's thumb, and he can be a bully if you don't stand up to him."

Drina blinked. "He's always been charming to me."

Scott regarded her sardonically. "But you haven't known him very long, have you? Underneath that pleasant façade he can be quite ruthless."

"I don't think you ought to criticize him to me," said Drina indignantly, "and if that's the opinion you hold of him I wonder you care to go on living in his house."

"I go on living in his house because it happens to suit both of us. We understand each other very well. How is the book progressing?"

Drina bit her lip. That was a decided snub, but she supposed she'd asked for it.

"I'm only on the preliminary sorting yet," she said stiffly, "but I'm finding it very interesting. I imagine there will be a lot of research before we can really start."

"I'm sure there will," said Scott so blandly that she could have hit him, and she rounded a corner with a squeal of tyres which infuriated her. Then she took a grip on herself and finished the journey into Canterbridge in impeccable style.

"Where is the garage?" she asked.

"You turn left at the end of Main Street, but if you're going to Smith's your best plan will be to park on the Market Square and we can both walk from there. Turn right at the next set of lights."

The parking ground at the far end of the Market Square was already quite full, but Scott guided Drina into a vacant space. As they walked out of the parking ground together he said: "Have you any other shopping to do after Smith's?"

"I've one or two odds and ends to buy for your aunt, and I need several things myself."

"I think you'll find all you want in Main Street. Smith's is half way down on the left-hand side and then—"

"Scott!" said a husky voice behind them. "I didn't expect to run into you here this morning. You knew I was back in circulation, didn't you?"

"Vanessa!" Scott wheeled round, and so did Drina. There, facing them, was a tall, slender girl with hair of a lovely red-gold and eyes as green as a cat's. There was something feline about the shape of her face too, with its high cheekbones and pointed chin, but she was strikingly attractive and her dark green suede trouser suit had been cut by a master hand. Drina was immediately conscious that her own tan jersey suit was last year's, and hadn't cost a quarter as much.

Vanessa held out both hands, and Scott took them in his.

"It's been a long time," she murmured.

"A very long time," he agreed, "and I haven't had much news of you."

"No. After I married Rico . . . but that's all in the past. You're still living at Broomyates and—not married?"

Her glance flickered to Drina, and Scott said: "No, not married. This is Drina Tonbridge, my father's secretary. She drove me here today because my car's in dock and I'm going to pick it up. Drina, this is Vanessa Mantaressi."

"I hear your father is semi-retired."

"Yes. He's prone to attacks of bronchitis, and has to take things rather more easily these days. Drina drives him to the factory in the mornings."

"I see. Let's go and have some coffee or a drink, Scott, and get up to date."

"Why not?"

"I must carry on with my shopping," said Drina hastily.

"Then we won't hold you up," said Vanessa sweetly. She slipped her arm through Scott's. "Is the White Swan still the best place?"

"I think so, in spite of the fact that we've acquired a restaurant and several coffee bars since you were here last."

Drina didn't wait for any more, but turned and made her way into Main Street. So that was the girl to whom Scott had been engaged. She was certainly lovely, and now that she was a widow there didn't seem any reason why they shouldn't come together again. What could have parted them in the first place?

As soon as her shopping was finished, Drina didn't stop for coffee herself but drove back to Broomyates. It was a sunny morning, and the light breeze was scattering the first leaves of autumn on the grass. Elfrida was cutting roses, so when she had put the car away Drina joined her.

"Aren't they perfect?" said the older woman, carefully gathering three half-open buds of Summer Holiday. "It's such a vibrant red, the kind of colour I've always longed to wear but never could. Did you pick up Father's books?"

"All but one, and Smith's said that would probably be in on Monday. We met Mrs. Mantaressi on the Market Square."

"Oh dear, but it was inevitable sooner or later," murmured Elfrida uneasily. "I do hope—that is, surely it can't cause trouble after all these years, their friendship, I mean, but she does belong to that family, and Father could never forget—" She sounded quite distracted, then made a palpable effort to pull herself together. "I'm being stupid, and you must wonder what I'm rambling about. I knew Vanessa and Scott were bound to meet before long, but I pushed it to the back of my mind. You see, there are complications, but I'd better tell you the whole story. It's common knowledge in the village, so there's no point in trying to keep it secret."

"Don't tell me anything you'd rather not," said Drina gently.

"It's just that I hoped Vanessa would never return here after her mother died, and I can't understand why she has done. You see, she was a baby when the family came to Lindisthorpe, and her father was taken on at the factory as a designer, but when she was four years old and Scott was six, her father ran away with

Scott's mother. Naturally, it was the talk of the village, and Vanessa's mother would have been left very badly off if Father hadn't helped her. He paid for Vanessa's education, and she and Scott grew up together. Then Scott went away to school, and they didn't see much of each other until he came home to work in the factory. Vanessa was eighteen and he was twenty when they fell madly in love. They were such a handsome couple."

"Was that when they became engaged?"

"Yes. Father couldn't prevent that, but he wouldn't give his consent to their marriage. Instead he sent Scott to Sweden for six months to study modern furniture design, and while he was away Vanessa went to Italy. She was wild to get into films, and Father was able to wangle her an introduction to an Italian film director who gave her a small part in one of his productions. I think she made three films altogether, and then she married a wealthy Italian business man, much older than herself. Soon after that her mother died, and Vanessa's never been back to the village since. Of course all the older people remember what happened, which is why I'm surprised she returned here. I don't think she should have done. It isn't fair on Scott."

"Was he very much upset at losing her?"

"Yes, very, though it's difficult to tell what Scott's feeling, he's so reserved. That comes of losing his mother so tragically. When she went away, he was quite old enough to remember her clearly. I could never understand how she could desert him like that; it changed him a great deal."

"I suppose her husband divorced her."

"There wasn't time. Three months later she and Vanessa's father were killed in a car crash in France, so Scott never saw her again. Unfortunately, he and his father were never close. My brother was always in uncommunicative man, and after the tragedy he became almost completely withdrawn and ignored Scott. I did my best, but I couldn't take his mother's place. Then for him to lose Vanessa too; it's no wonder he's held aloof from women since. I'm afraid he's still in love with her, and couldn't bear to put anyone in her place."

"It wouldn't be surprising," acknowledged Drina. "She's extremely beautiful. I don't know whether her hair colour's natural or not, but it's the most glorious red-gold and her clothes are fabulous. She certainly stood out in Canterbridge."

"If she and Scott come together, it will cause trouble. Father thought it was his duty to do what he could for her, but he never liked the family, and I'm sure he won't want Scott to marry her, any more than he did before."

"But Scott's old enough now to please himself."

"Yes, so it's no use my worrying, only I can't help it. What time is it, Drina? I must go and set the table for lunch, and make sure that Mrs. Braine's on time with it. Father does hate it not being ready promptly at one o'clock."

Elfrida hurried away, and Drina went up to her room. One of the cleaning women was polishing the hall floor in a desultory fashion, and Drina hoped that Mr. Carlyon wouldn't notice her and make remarks at lunch about her lack of energy. There were three women who came to Broomyates two days a week each because Mrs. Braine refused to do anything at all but cook. Elfrida coped with the housekeeping and the shopping, but she wasn't methodical and exasperated her father by her poor organization. Unobtrusively

56

Drina tried to do what she could, but she was afraid of her employer being even more cross if he found out.

Now, as she was washing her hands and brushing her hair, she pondered over what Elfrida had told her. Scott had certainly had a raw deal from life, and perhaps it wasn't surprising that he distrusted women. Still, he was surely mature enough to realize that they weren't all cut to one pattern. Drina still smarted at the memory of the things he had said to her, and told herself that no matter how shabbily he had been treated she really couldn't like him.

The days began to fly by. Drina was kept busy compiling copious notes for the book from a huge pile of volumes Mr. Carlyon had sent down from London. She began to be fascinated by the material she was amassing, and to understand how the various styles of furniture had evolved. If she had any time to spare, Elfrida welcomed her help, and as a labour of love she was cleaning and polishing the drawing-room furniture. The pieces were so beautiful that she didn't like to see them dull and neglected, and it gave her a real pleasure to bring out the patina of the wood by a vigorous application of elbow grease.

When she had been at Broomyates nearly a fortnight Lois wrote to say that she and Marc were returning to England. Nothing had worked out as they had hoped. Marc was finding it increasingly difficult to make a living, and their money was running out. For the time being, they would be staying in a cheap hotel in London—"just until we can find a flat", wrote Lois. "It's the Cayetuna in Bloomsbury, so you can write to me there. You seem to have fallen on your feet; I only wish Marc would find a cushy job. He's very depressed at the way things have turned out."

Her job wasn't exactly cushy, thought Drina wryly, even though she was enjoying it. She was discovering that Mr. Carlyon wasn't quite so easy to work for as she had imagined. He became very put out if he were crossed in the slightest way, and she soon learned not to make any suggestions even if she believed they would be helpful. What she missed most was company of her own age. She liked Elfrida, but they belonged to different generations, and she had little contact with Scott. She reminded herself that she had come to Broomyates to work, not to lead a gay social life, but it would have been pleasant to have had someone to go out with in the evenings, to take her to an occasional dance or theatre.

She had seen no more of Vanessa Mantaressi since that first encounter, but that wasn't to say she and Scott weren't meeting away from the house. Vanessa had rented Old Lodge, a period cottage owned by some people who were spending a year abroad, and according to the gossip Drina had picked up in the Post Office, spent most of her time driving furiously through the lanes in her yellow sports car. Elfrida was careful never to mention Vanessa's name when her father was near, and Scot never referred to her at all, so Drina had no idea how the situation lay between them.

Sally Hurdlow was due to be married at the beginning of October and invited Drina to the wedding, so she asked Mr. Carlyon if she might have a weekend off.

"Certainly," he said. "Enjoy yourself, and don't bother coming back until Monday morning. Have you anywhere to stay after the wedding?"

"Sally's invited me to use the flat since she and Andy will be away for a week. My sister will be in London then, so I thought I might take the opportunity of seeing her as well."

"Oh yes, you were telling me that she'd been living abroad. What are she and her husband planning to do now?"

"I don't really know. Marc was an art student, and he was invited out to Ibiza to do some murals in a restaurant a friend of his was running. He hoped it would lead to other commissions, but apparently they haven't materialized."

"Mm. Has he any talent for furniture design? We could do with another designer at the factory."

"May I mention that to him? He could be interested."

Drina was to go up to London on the Friday evening by train, but the problem was how to get to Canterbridge station. She could have driven herself there in the car, but that would have meant her leaving it at the station and there was no one to pick it up.

"If only I'd learned to drive," lamented Elfrida, then she brightened. "Scott will take you, I'm sure. He doesn't usually stay late at the factory on Fridays, so there'll be plenty of time for you to catch the seven o'clock train."

That wasn't what Drina wanted at all. "There's no need for me to trouble him. Surely I can hire a taxi in the village?"

"Joe Sparrow has one, but he's ill at the moment. His brother-in-law sometimes helps him out," began Elfrida.

"Then I'll get hold of him. Don't worry, I'll manage somehow."

But before she could make enquiries about Joe Sparrow's brother-in-law, Elfrida announced triumphantly that it was all settled.

"I had a word with Scott, and he can easily run you to Canterbridge on Friday evening."

Drina swallowed her annoyance. Elfrida had meant it for the best, but if only she hadn't interfered. Now Drina was condemned to a strained journey with Scott. Thank goodness, it wouldn't last long.

Curiously enough, it started off very amicably. For once the sardonic expression Scott usually wore was missing, and he seemed relaxed. When she tried to thank him for the lift, he dismissed it with a smile.

"As it happens, I was going into Canterbridge anyway."

"But not before your dinner, surely?"

"No, later on, but now I've decided to have a meal there. It will be more convenient. This friend who's going to be married, is she the one who shared the flat with you?"

"Yes. The wedding wouldn't have taken place quite so soon if I hadn't left the flat free for her husband and herself. He's with a chemical firm, and hopes to get promotion before long."

"And what will you do with yourself after the wedding?"

"I'm not quite sure. My sister and her husband will be in London, so I'll probably go and see them on Sunday."

"And what about Don?"

"Don Madderley? What about him?"

"Haven't you told him you'll be in London over the weekend?"

"No, I haven't."

Scott raised his eyebrows. "I thought you'd be making the most of your opportunities."

Drina felt herself go red. "Don and I were good friends on the cruise, but I haven't seen or heard from him since."

"I'm surprised."

Scott's voice was frankly unbelieving, and Drina retaliated by saying: "I haven't run into Mrs. Mantaressi in the village, but perhaps she does all her shopping in Canterbridge."

"I imagine she does most of it in London or Italy. She's been in Rome settling some business affairs of her husband's and arrived back in London yesterday. She's coming down to Canterbridge by train tonight."

"And you're meeting her?"

"Yes."

Now she understood why it was no trouble for him to take her, Drina, to the station, and why he was in a good mood. Obviously he and Vanessa had been communicating with each other, and the only reason Drina hadn't seen them together was because Vanessa had been away. She was glad that the train was already standing in so that Scott could find her a seat and then leave her. Once the train was moving, she leaned back in her corner, and resolved to enjoy herself during the weekend without a thought for Broomyates and its inhabitants.

Sally greeted her enthusiastically, and showed her the alterations she and Andy had made to the flat.

"Not that I can hope to impress you," she said, "living as you are in the lap of luxury."

"I wouldn't call it exactly that. Broomyates is a big house, but it isn't easy to run and Miss Carlyon has to do quite a lot herself."

"Well, anyway it's lovely to have you here. Mummy and Daddy will be along later on. They're staying at the Cranfield Hotel."

"Were they disappointed that you decided not to be married from home?"

"Mummy was at first, but then she admitted that it would have been difficult to transport Andy's horde of relations over to Ireland. Come and look at the presents. We've got masses of stuff. Heaven knows where I'm going to store it."

Nothing marred the wedding. It was a golden day, and Sally made a radiant bride in parchment crêpe with Andy's sister for bridesmaid in flame velvet. When the happy couple had departed for a honeymoon in Malta Mr. and Mrs. Hurdlow, Sally's parents, came back to the flat with Drina before flying home to Ireland, Mrs. Hurdlow declaring that she was dying for a good cup of tea. After they had left, Drina tidied up, and then finding herself surprisingly tired had an early night.

She took the Tube the next day to Bloomsbury, and found the hotel where Lois and Marc were staying. It was very modest, even shabby, and she wasn't surprised that Lois was anxious to hustle her out of the dingy lounge.

"Come up to our room," said Lois. "It's like a morgue in here."

"Where's Marc?"

"He's gone into the city to see if any of his old friends can put something in his way. So far there's been nothing doing."

"What went wrong in Ibiza? I thought you were enjoying the life out there."

"So we were at first, but there weren't the openings we'd been led to expect and although Marc painted murals which were commissioned, he was paid only half the fees he'd been promised because Steven said he couldn't afford any more. Then accommodation was difficult to rent, so in the end we'd no choice but to come home."

"What are you going to do now?"

Lois shrugged. "Wait for something to turn up. I've

been trying for modelling jobs, but I've lost contact with the photographers I knew. I suppose your Mr. Carlyon couldn't put anything our way?"

"We were speaking of you before I left," admitted Drina, "and he mentioned there was room for someone in the design section at the factory, but I wasn't sure whether it would appeal to Marc."

"Why shouldn't it?" cried Lois. "And even if it didn't, once we're down there there could be other opportunities. Where would we live? Is there anywhere to rent in the village?"

"I don't know of anywhere, that's what's worrying me, but you might find rooms in Canterbridge, though it would mean a five-mile bus journey for Marc every day."

"I'm sure he wouldn't mind that, and perhaps we could afford a second-hand car," said Lois optimistically. "Now tell me all about the Carlyons, and what the house is like."

Before long Marc came in, a worried frown furrowing his brow. He looked older, and though she had never thought it was sensible of him and Lois to get married so impulsively, Drina felt sorry for him. Certainly all his dreams of a life in the sun had vanished, and when she mentioned Mr. Carlyon's offer he seized on it eagerly.

"I don't know anything about furniture designing, but I'd be glad to give it a trial," he said. "At least, it would be something in the arts line, and better than sweeping the streets, which is what I'll be reduced to if I don't find a job soon."

"I'll speak to Mr. Carlyon the moment I get back and ring you right away," promised Drina.

She kept her word, and Robert Carlyon repeated his offer to give Marc a trial.

"If he's willing to work hard, and he has a spark of originality, he could carve out a successful career for himself," he said. "How soon can he start?"

"The moment they can find somewhere to live. I was wondering if one of the men at the factory has accommodation to spare."

"We can do better than that. There's the stable flat standing empty," and then, as Drina looked mystified, he added: "That flat over the garages in what was the old stable block. We had it fixed up for a married couple who were working here as cook and gardener-handyman, and it could soon be made habitable again. There's plenty of furniture in the attics which could be used."

Elfrida was only too pleased to show Drina over the stable flat which consisted of a sitting-room, kitchen, bedroom, minute bathroom and even minuter boxroom. As her father had said, there was plenty of spare furniture in the attics so that the flat could be made quite comfortable. Drina rang Marc, and it was arranged that he and Lois should come down in a week's time which would give Drina and Elfrida a chance to air beds and put up curtains.

Drina felt apprehensive about Scott's reaction to the news. The design department was very much his baby, and she was afraid that he would resent Marc being wished upon him. She waited for him to bring up the subject, and when he remained silent she plunged into it herself.

"It was very kind of your grandfather to give Marc the chance of a job in the factory. I know Marc appreciates it."

"Let's hope his talent's equal to his gratitude,"

said Scott sarcastically. "I can't afford passengers, however philanthropic my grandfather's feeling."

Drina winced. How hateful of him to draw attention to that. She hadn't set out to wheedle this job for Marc, but nothing and no one would ever convince Scott of that.

CHAPTER FOUR

THE next afternoon, returning from the village where she had been to post letters for Mr. Carlyon, Drina saw a sleek yellow sports car outside the door, so it wasn't difficult to guess who the visitor was. She crept into the hall, meaning to slip up to her room, but Elfrida came out of the drawing-room and greeted her with relief.

"Oh, Drina, do go in there and talk to Vanessa. You know I've no small talk, and Scott isn't back from the factory yet, so Father's entertaining her and I'm afraid he may grow bored. I must see how dinner's getting on. If she doesn't leave soon I'll have to ask her to stay to the meal, but I hope she'll refuse."

Drina went into the drawing-room where Vanessa was lying back in one corner of the sofa, her long boots of chestnut calf making a pleasing contrast to her yellow tweed skirt. Robert Carlyon said: "This is my secretary, Drina Tonbridge; Drina, this is Vanessa Mantaressi," and Vanessa smiled brilliantly.

"We've met before, in Canterbridge one morning."

"Yes," agreed Drina. "I drove Scott in because his car was being overhauled."

Vanessa cast a glance at the door. "Does he usually work so late? I was sure he'd be home by now."

"We've a special export order in and he wanted to pass it himself for dispatch," said Mr. Carlyon easily. "Scott's very conscientious, as I expect you remember."

"Only too well," answered Vanessa sweetly. "If you hadn't persuaded him that it was his duty to go to Sweden . . . but it never does to mull over the past, does it? It's the future which counts."

Robert Carlyon smiled. "Very true."

There was a feeling of tension in the air, and Drina thought they measured glances like old adversaries. She also conceded that Vanessa Mantaressi was easily the most attractive woman she had ever seen, and that Vanessa was well aware of it.

The atmosphere in the room changed as Elfrida came back to report that Scott had just arrived home and that dinner was ready. She looked awkwardly at Vanessa who smiled blandly back but gave no indication of leaving, so that Elfrida was obliged to say: "Will you stay and have dinner with us, Vanessa?"

"I'd love to," answered Vanessa. "Perhaps I could tidy up first."

"Yes, of course," said Elfrida. "Drina—" but before Drina could step forward, Vanessa laughed.

"No need to show me the way. I know this house so well, unless the bathrooms have been changed in the last few years."

Elfrida flushed. "It was stupid of me to forget. The nearest one's at the head of the stairs as it always was."

Drina sped up to her room, and came down to find all the others in the dining-room, except for Vanessa who clearly intended to make an entrance. She succeeded in drawing everyone's eye on her as she hesitated in the doorway, but Drina, watching Scott's face, found it impossible to tell whether or not he was pleased to see her. Certainly he came forward to greet her, and she smiled radiantly at him.

"Scott, at last! I was beginning to think that you'd

67

decided to stay at the factory all night and that I'd have to leave without seeing you."

"I'm glad I turned up in time," he answered. "Will you sit here"

Mrs. Braine thumped plates and a tureen of soup down on the other side of the hatch, and Scott carried them to the table. Vanessa ate two spoonfuls, then pushed away her plate.

"Scott," she said, "I'm so bored up in that house by myself. I must find something to do. You've some scheme afoot for building a community centre on that meadow land adjoining your garden, haven't you? The woman who comes to clean for me told me about it."

"Yes. The present Village Hall's far too small for the needs of the village now, and I was told some time ago that the field beyond the garden here might be for sale. Now I've signed the contract to buy it and I'll present it to the village, but the cost of the new hall is to be met by public effort. We're having a meeting on Saturday to elect a committee and decide how to go about our fund-raising. I want this to be a real community project so that everyone can feel he has a share in it."

"Is the meeting open to everyone?"

"Yes."

"Then I'll come to it and see what I can do to help."

"Do you mean to settle down here permanently?" asked Elfrida. "I should have thought it would seem rather tame after living in Rome."

"I haven't quite made up my mind what to do," returned Vanessa. "After Rico's death I had to reorganize my life. He liked me to entertain for his friends, so we tended to live in a whirl, but when he died everything changed and I needed time to come to terms with myself. That's why I decided to return here for a while at least. I'm still English, even if I have lived in Italy for the last six years, and this was where I was brought up and where I have my roots."

For the rest of the meal she reminisced about her childhood, addressing herself almost exclusively to Scott, and when they'd drunk their coffee she got up to go. Scott went out to her car with her, and was away quite a time. Mr. Carlyon retired to his study, and Drina went up to her room. She felt curiously restless and would have liked to go for a long walk, but she couldn't wander round in the dark, so in the end she had to return to the sitting-room.

The meeting to discuss how to raise the money for the community centre was to be held in the Village Hall on Saturday evening. Scott was to be chairman of the proceedings and Elfrida was to go with him, but Robert Carlyon declared that he was too old to be involved in new projects.

"Are you coming?" Elfrida asked Drina.

Drina hesitated. "Well, I don't work at the factory and I'm not a member of the village, so I don't know whether I'm entitled to be there."

"I'd be glad if you'd take some notes," said Scott. "I need someone reliable to keep a record of the meeting."

"Thank you for the compliment."

"Oh, I've never doubted that you were a competent shorthand-typist," he retorted, giving the impression that all his suspicions of her lay in other directions.

On Saturday evening he drove Drina and his aunt to the Village Hall where there was evidently enthusiasm for his project, since the place was full. Scott took his seat on the platform together with the Vicar, and Drina was accommodated with a small table to one side where she could rest her shorthand notebook.

Scott explained his aims in a crisp speech which went over very well. Drina had to admire the clarity with which he put his plans forward and his sincerity in wanting everyone to enjoy the amenities of a centre. He told his audience that while he would buy and donate the land the village would be responsible for building costs, and it was the raising of this money that they were concerned with tonight. It was proposed to set up a committee of six to discuss ways and means, and nominations for members would be considered now.

The Vicar and Scott were proposed and seconded immediately, followed by the butcher in the High Street, the new headmistress of the village school, and a local farmer. Then there was a pause until a man jumped up and said: "I propose Mrs. Mantaressi," and a woman at the end of the row called: "I second that."

A murmur ran through the hall, and the Vicar said: "Mrs. Mantaressi has been proposed and seconded. All those in favour."

Several hands shot into the air and Drina saw that Vanessa was sitting at the back, looking very striking in bright red.

The Vicar said: "Any more nominations? No? Then we have our six committee members."

It was decided that the committee should meet next Saturday evening at Broomyates, and in the meantime suggestions for the raising of money would be welcomed. There were a surprising number of these which Drina noted down, and on the committee agreeing to consider them all, the meeting broke up.

Vanessa joined them, saying: "Wasn't it kind of them to elect me, and so unexpected. Still, I mean to do my utmost to help to raise that money. I've all kinds of ideas, Scott. Come back with me, and we'll discuss them over a drink."

"I'm driving my aunt and Drina home," he said.

"Of course, if they'd like to come back for a drink as well, I'd be only too happy," declared Vanessa, but Elfrida said : "Thank you, but I've several things to see to."

"Well, couldn't Drina drive you in Scott's car and I'll run him back myself?"

Drina looked at Scott, and Vanessa said impatiently : "What are we waiting for?"

"If Scott doesn't mind my driving his car," began Drina, sure that he'd never trust her with it, but to her surprise he said : "Why not? From what I've seen, you drive very competently. Here are the keys," and he handed them to her.

For a moment Drina was silent with astonishment, then she stammered : "Thank you."

Vanessa slipped her arm through Scott's as they walked through the hall and out to where the cars were parked. She drove out in fine style while Drina was testing the unfamiliar controls, and Elfrida said : "You're honoured. Scott wouldn't trust his car to any-one."

"I realize that. I certainly never expected him to lend it to me."

"But you're a good driver."

"So's Mrs. Mantaressi."

"I suppose she is. Oh dear, I wish I could like her better, but I never really cared for her when she used to come here before. I'm sorry she's back because I was beginning to hope that Scott had got over her. Now he'll fall under her spell all over again."

"The village must have fallen under it too, to elect her to the committee."

"I'm not so sure of that. The man who proposed her keeps the garage at the corner of Main Street and the woman who seconded him cleans for her. I was wondering if she'd dropped them both a strong hint that she'd like to be on the committee and would make it worth their while if they helped her to achieve her ambition. I'm convinced that she wants to be in the centre of things, and doesn't really care about the welfare of the village."

Drina was of the same opinion, and believed that Vanessa was determined to impress Scott. She was clearly making a play for him, and it would take a very strong-minded man to resist her charm.

Lois and Marc arrived the following day, and in the meantime, the other two had been hard at work making the stable flat habitable, Elfrida having produced rugs and curtains to harmonize with the furniture.

"Do you think your sister would prefer these blue curtains in the sitting-room or the bedroom?" she asked.

"The sitting-room, I think, because it gets more sun," answered Drina, "but I can manage to hang them on my own if there are other things you want to do."

"No, I'm enjoying myself. It's fun furnishing a small place, but Broomyates overwhelms me," sighed Elfrida. "Naturally, Father would never live anywhere else and I can understand that, but if only I'd had the opportunity to get away. My mother died when I was sixteen, and it was taken for granted that I would housekeep for my father, so I thought it was my duty to stay at home."

"What would you have done if you'd had your choice?" asked Drina.

"Learned flower arranging under someone like

Constance Spry. I've done my best to teach myself through books, but if only I could have made a career of it I know I'd have succeeded. Still, it wasn't to be, and it's no use dwelling on the past."

Poor Elfrida, thought Drina. All those wasted, frustrated years when she might have been doing work she loved.

Lois and Marc arrived in a taxi from Canterbridge, and Lois professed herself delighted with the stable flat. Marc was sincere in his thanks to Drina for all she'd done.

"I did very little," she told him. "It was Mr. Carlyon's idea."

"I'm very grateful to him, too, and I mean to make a go of this job." He smiled wryly. "I thought life would be all sunshine and roses in Ibiza, but I soon found I was wrong. It's one thing to exist on a shoestring when you're single, but quite another when you've got a wife to support."

He was thinner, and there were lines of strain around his mouth, but Drina found herself liking him much better than when he and Lois were married. Then he had been brash and self-confident, intolerant of any point of view which clashed with his own, and contemptuous of people with nine-to-five jobs. He'd changed a lot, and not for the worse, she thought.

"Oh, you worry too much," said Lois gaily. "I'm going to enjoy myself and find a job. I want some new clothes."

Marc frowned. "I can buy you clothes."

"It isn't only that. I should be bored to death on my own here all day. Is there a bus service to Canterbridge, Drina?"

"Yes, half-hourly."

"Then I'll look for work there."

As it happened, she had no need to seek a job in Canterbridge. She and Drina were strolling in the garden after dinner that evening when the yellow sports car shot up the drive and Vanessa got out. She caught sight of Drina, and directing a look full of curiosity at Lois, strolled up to them.

"Hallo," she said. "Enjoying the evening air?"

"Yes," answered Drina, and introduced Lois.

"So you've joined your sister," commented Vanessa, and turned to Drina. "Is Scott anywhere about?"

"I'm afraid not. He went into Canterbridge immediately after dinner."

Vanessa looked annoyed. "What a nuisance! I was hoping he might be able to tell me of a good carpenter, perhaps a man in the factory who does odd jobs in his spare time."

"Is it something in the house you want fixing?"

"No, I've taken the lease of a boutique in Canterbridge, and I want some fitments putting up."

"A boutique?" echoed Drina. "But I thought—"

"Oh, I'm not running it to make money but to give myself an interest. I've a flair for clothes, and I thought it would be amusing to see if I could sell them. I'm going to advertise for an assistant, and we'll run the place between us."

"Would I do?" asked Lois boldly.

Vanessa stared at her appraisingly. "Do you know anything about the rag trade?"

"I've done some modelling, and I'm interested in clothes."

"Well I don't suppose there's much choice of personnel in Canterbridge," drawled Vanessa, "so I'll give you a trial. Come and see me tomorrow afternoon. The premises are at the bottom of Main Street on the left-hand side."

"Thank you," answered Lois.

"I shan't hang on in the hope of seeing Scott. I'll give him a ring later."

When she had gone, Lois turned jubilantly to her sister.

"How's that for initiative? I've fixed myself up with a job in the first few hours I've been here."

"I hope you like it," said Drina cautiously. "I don't imagine Mrs. Mantaressi is the easiest person to work for."

"If we don't suit each other I'll look for something else. Come on, let's go into the flat and make some coffee."

Lois went into Canterbridge the next day and found the boutique. Vanessa had contacted Scott who had recommended a joiner to her and the man had already commenced work, urged on by Vanessa's promise of generous payment if he had all the fitments in place by the end of the week. She had already been in touch with wholesalers, and had arranged for goods to be delivered during the next few days. Lois was impressed by her businesslike attitude, and told Drina that Canterbridge would soon be sitting up and taking notice.

"It's what the place needs," she declared. "There isn't a decent dress shop in the main street. As soon as we're fully stocked you must come in, Drina. You could do with a new outfit."

"I spent a lot on clothes for the cruise," pointed out Drina, "so I can't afford much this winter. Still, I would like a dress for Christmas, so I'll call in later on and see what you've got."

Marc too seemed to have settled down satisfactorily at the factory. He didn't say much about it, but he was obviously interested in his work, and the strain had left his face. The days went by, and the next meeting of the community centre committee drew near. Vanessa hadn't been to Broomyates during the week, but she rang up and apologized for neglecting them, saying that there had been such a lot to do getting the boutique launched that she had been tired out every night but that she would certainly be at the meeting, and would come early so as to have a little chat first. Elfrida took this call as Scott was out, and said apprehensively to Drina: "Oh dear, I do hope Scott's here when she arrives, otherwise I can see myself having to make laborious conversation which won't suit either of us."

"What won't suit either of you?" enquired Scott, coming in at that moment, and she answered: "Vanessa's coming early to the meeting tomorrow, so you must be here to greet her. You know how bad I am at playing hostess."

"She won't bite," said Scott good-humouredly, "but don't worry, I'll be here. By the way, Drina, do you mind sitting in on these meetings and acting as secretary? I'd like to get things on a straightforward footing from the beginning without arguments later on about figures, and who said what. If proper minutes are taken, then we can refer to them. You're not doing anything tomorrow evening, are you?"

"No, I'm not, so I don't mind attending the meeting."

"Good. After this, we probably shan't be holding them more than once a month, so it won't be a very onerous task."

Vanessa was the first to arrive in an emerald green dress under a beaver jacket. She looked stunning, and Drina didn't wonder that Scott couldn't take his eyes off her.

"This is all going to be fun," said Vanessa gaily, accepting a glass of sherry. "I've got lots of ideas for making money, Scott. You'll be able to have your centre in no time."

"Good. This sounds like some of the others."

It proved to be the headmistress, and she was rapidly followed by the butcher and the farmer, with the Vicar bringing up the rear.

"I'm so sorry," he said. "I was delayed by a caller just as I was about to set out."

They were soon all seated round the dining-room table, and Scott as chairman opened the proceedings. Vanessa immediately launched into a series of money-making schemes, most of which were far too ambitious in scope and were received by the others in a dubious silence.

"I don't really think we'd be able to cope with the kind of arts festival you suggest," ventured Joan Priddy, the headmistress. "I mean, the church is a fine Norman foundation, but after that there really isn't anything of particular interest in the village to bring people here."

"And if we have an historical pageant, who's going to pay for the costumes?" demanded the butcher. "No sense in putting on something which swallows all the profits in hiring fees."

"I thought the Mothers' Union could run a Sale of Work," suggested the Vicar. "That usually wins popular support."

"Ah, a Sale of Work," agreed the butcher. "You know where you are with that."

"Oh well, if you're determined to be unenterprising." Vanessa's mouth took on a sulky curve and she leaned back in her chair as if she didn't intend to take any further interest in the proceedings.

"A Sale of Work then, run by the Mothers' Union," said Scott imperturbably. "Any other ideas?"

"I thought we might make a collection of waste

paper," said Joan Priddy. "A friend of mine teaches in a school where they managed to send their school choir to one of the European music festivals by the sale of waste paper. You can obtain quite a high price per ton for it."

"That sounds a practical scheme," said Scott. "If the school children would help with the collecting, we might make a nice sum. We'd have to circularize all the houses in the village, and I don't see why we shouldn't do the same in Canterbridge if we could get someone with a car to go the rounds. Vanessa?"

For a moment Drina thought she was going to refuse, then she smiled charmingly. "Of course. We ought to have cards printed which we could drop through people's letter-boxes, telling them that we'd call on a certain day."

"Yes, that would be a good idea. I'll have a batch run off on the duplicator at the factory."

No more suggestions were forthcoming, so the committee broke up, Scott announcing that the next meeting would be in a month's time when they could report on the progress which had been made. Vanessa lingered behind and followed Drina and Scott into the sitting-room where Elfrida and her father were installed.

"Oh, is the meeting over?" enquired Elfrida. "I'll go and make some coffee. I expect you need it after all that talking."

"They're so hidebound," sighed Vanessa, sinking into a chair. "No more original ideas emerged than a Sale of Work, and everything I suggested was vetoed."

"I thought the plan for collecting waste paper was a good scheme," remarked Drina. "Everybody can feel they've contributed to that, even the small children.

78

I'm willing to distribute cards if you want any more volunteers."

"We need as many as we can get," said Scott. "When it comes to collecting the paper itself, I can arrange to borrow a van from the factory. We'll have to go the rounds on a definite evening each month and draw up a rota of collectors."

"Put me down for it," said Drina, and Vanessa broke in quickly: "And me. I'm willing to do my share whatever's decided, but I did hope we might have tried something a little more ambitious, and I still think an historical pageant is a good idea."

"Historical pageant!" snorted Robert Carlyon when she had gone. "I suppose she sees herself as Cleopatra." He looked obliquely at Scott. "We're not Super-Colossal Films here."

"Some of her ideas were good ones," pointed out Scott, "only Vanessa doesn't quite realize the limitations of a place the size of Lindisthorpe."

"I wish I could do something to help Scott's scheme," said Elfrida wistfully as she and Drina washed the coffee cups. "Something individual, not merely helping to collect waste paper."

"I believe you could," answered Drina. "It came to me when Miss Priddy mentioned the church as the village's one asset. Why not hold a Flower Festival there at Easter? I saw the one in Westminster Abbey a few years ago, and there have been others up and down the country. With your gift for arranging flowers, I'm sure you could make the church look beautiful, and with plenty of publicity in Canterbridge you'd get a lot of people coming out to look at it on the Bank Holiday as well as the Sunday. If you charged an entrance fee, I'm sure you'd make a profit."

"Do you think I could?" gasped Elfrida, suspending

operations in her excitement. "I'd have to find out a lot about running an event like that, but I know where I could get the information."

"Then why not try? Mention it to Scott, and ask him to propose it at the next committee meeting."

"Oh yes, I could do that, but I'd have to work out facts and figures, and then there'd be the question of obtaining the flowers. I don't know whether the market in Canterbridge could cope."

Drina left her talking confusedly but happily to herself, and hoped that she had done the right thing. She very much wanted Elfrida to have the glory of achieving something on her own. It would give her some badly needed confidence.

On Monday Drina drove Mr. Carlyon as usual to the factory and arrived at lunchtime to pick him up. She tapped on his office door and went in, only to find that Scott was there talking rapidly to his grandfather.

"Here she is," said Robert Carlyon genially. "I'm sure she'll be only too ready to oblige."

"Oblige in what way?" Drina looked from one to the other of them.

"My secretary's gone home with migraine," said Scott, "and I've an important specification which must be typed this afternoon. There are other typists here, but none as experienced as Miss Birkdale, and this work needs someone who really knows her job and won't make any mistakes even though the figures are complicated. Grandfather says that your typing is first class, and has offered to lend you to me this afternoon if you're willing."

"Certainly," said Drina. "Do you want me to start now?"

"Not without any lunch. Take my grandfather

home, have your lunch, and I'll send a car for you at two o'clock. All right?"

"Of course."

Drina found that she was looking forward to the afternoon. It would be interesting to have a change of work, also she was curious to see Scott Carlyon's office. It proved to be austerely furnished with the comfortable but supremely elegant chairs which she remembered remarking on in the boardroom of the oil company.

"Oh," she said impulsively, "you've got them here—the chairs, I mean."

"You've seen them before?"

"Yes. I had a temporary job with Universal Oils, and when I admired the furniture in the boardroom my boss told me that you'd designed it."

"So I did." Scott looked amused. "It was my first industrial commission, and I was inordinately proud of it. I refused to compromise on the chairs because to make them higher would have spoilt the sculptured line, so I had to design the boardroom table lower than usual."

"Well, the ebonised wood looked very effective against the white walls. I remember thinking that when I could afford a place of my own I'd have one of those chairs in the hall."

"I'm flattered, though I must admit that I have an affection for them myself because they made my name. Now, shall we start work? I'll explain the layout of the specification to you, and then leave you to get on with it."

Drina found that he had spoken the truth when he said it was complicated. There was a bewildering mass of figures to be tabulated, and she thanked providence that the various jobs she'd taken had given her an insight into all forms of work. She typed busily away, only pausing for ten minutes to drink a cup of tea a junior brought her at four o'clock, and then at half-past five Scott came back to examine what she'd done.

"This is first class," he said approvingly. "Quite as good as Miss Birkdale would have produced. You can stop now, and thank you very much for all you've done."

"But there are still three pages to type," objected Drina.

"They'll have to wait until morning. Fortunately Miss Birkdale's migraines don't usually last long."

"I thought you wanted the specification completed tonight?"

"Yes, I did, but I realize it was too much to expect."

"I'd rather stay and complete it now that I've got so far. It won't take me very long."

"I'll admit I'd be grateful if you did. I'm staying on myself to finish reading some papers, so I'll pack it up and dispatch it."

He sat down with a sheaf of papers, and Drina carried on with her work. An hour later she spun the last sheet out of her typewriter, and straightened the pile of papers on the desk. Scott raised his head.

"Finished? Good, so have I. Perhaps you'd like to freshen up in my cloakroom, and then we'll go and have a meal. There's a new hotel opened on the other side of Canterbridge and they say the food's pretty good there. Like to sample it?"

Drina blinked at him. "Yes, I would, but we'd still be in time for dinner at Broomyates."

"I know we would, but I think we both deserve some relaxation. The cloakroom's through that door."

It was all primrose tiles and fluffy matching towels. Drina, making up her face in the generous sweep of mirror, wished that she had put on her amber suit instead of the charcoal jersey dress she was wearing, but she had had no idea that Scott would invite her out for a meal. She rejoined him, and together they walked to where his car was parked at the back of the building.

The hotel he had mentioned was about ten miles away, and had a huge log fire burning in the entrance hall where the bar was situated. After a dry sherry each they went into the dining-room where Drina sat back while the head waiter recommended the roast pheasant and conferred with Scott over the wine list.

"This is a charming place," remarked Drina as the soup arrived, "and I'm so glad there isn't any music. I'd much rather eat my meal in peace."

"So would I," agreed Scott, "but we're in the minority. I've come to the conclusion that the louder the noise the better most people like it."

"Long live the individualists!"

The claret Scott had ordered was expensively smooth, and gave Drina a deliciously glowing feeling. She found herself saying with real warmth: "I've never thanked you for giving Marc a chance in the design department, but I am grateful."

"There's no need to thank me since he's fitted in very well. Naturally he's groping a bit at first, but he has an instinctive feeling for wood and I think when he's grown used to using it as a medium he'll turn out some very good designs."

"Tell me how you came to start making furniture," said Drina impulsively. "How the firm was founded. I'm interested."

"Are you? Well, it started with my great-grandfather. He was a craftsman, and he made individual pieces for wealthy patrons who commissioned them. His workshop was the beginning of things, and then when my grandfather grew up he joined him. They both had a love of fine wood which I've inherited though, curiously enough, my father never had it. He went into the business on the administrative side, but he—"

Scott stopped short, and Drina followed the direction of his eyes. Entering the hotel dining-room with a dark, stocky man and looking breathtaking in a dress of tangerine wild silk and a mink jacket was Vanessa. At the same moment she caught sight of them, and for one brief instant Drina saw her expression alter. There was no mistaking the look of naked dislike Vanessa shot her, and it gave Drina a very unpleasant jolt.

CHAPTER FIVE

THE next instant Vanessa was smiling brilliantly and sweeping towards them.

"Hullo, Scott," she said. "I didn't know you were coming here tonight."

"Drina and I have been working late at the factory," he announced. "She's been helping me with an important specification, my own secretary having succumbed to a migraine."

"I see." The stocky man touched her arm, and Vanessa turned to him reluctantly.

"Carlo, I want you to meet a very old friend of mine, Scott Carlyon, and this is his father's secretary. Scott, this is Carlo Pacelli who is connected with the film company I used to work for. He's been trying to persuade me to go back to Italy and make another film, but I've been telling him I don't want to leave England."

"But why?" queried Carlo, shrugging expressively. "What is so attractive about this country with its terrible weather and equally terrible food?"

"Nonsense!" protested Vanessa laughingly. "Some of the food's very good. That's why I've brought you here so that you can sample it."

"Then let us make a start," said Carlo, putting a hand on her arm. "We have much to talk about."

"Oh, very well." Vanessa looked ruefully at Scott, and saying: "See you soon," allowed Carlo to lead her away.

Drina, smarting under the snub of being introduced

as Robert Carlyon's secretary as if she hadn't a name, said nothing. For a moment Scott remained silent too, then he remarked : "What were we talking about ?"

"How your business was built up. You were saying that your father had no feeling for wood."

"No, he hadn't. When I look back I don't think he can have been really interested in making furniture at all, but as you can imagine, my grandfather took it for granted that his son would go into the business."

"Yes. Did your grandfather specialize in anything ?"

"He was a pioneer of post-war unit furniture which was the salvation of the firm when things were difficult, and wood was in short supply. The pieces in your bedroom were some of the designs he developed after the family upheaval. I imagine my aunt told you that my mother ran away with Vanessa's father ?"

"She did mention it."

"It's no secret. Vanessa's father joined the firm when she was two years old and I was nearly four. I've heard that he was talented, but he didn't have much chance to prove himself because he and my mother ran away just over two years later. I can remember her quite plainly, but Vanessa has no real recollection of her father."

"It must have been dreadful for you to lose your mother at such an early age," said Drina sympathetically.

His face hardened. "I missed her very much at first, but I soon learned to adapt myself. So did Vanessa."

It made a bond between them which nothing can break, thought Drina, and suddenly the mound of whipped cream and chestnuts she was enjoying tasted as flat as cold rice pudding. Across the room Vanessa's dress glowed, and Carlo's swarthy face was bent attentively towards her. She had everything—looks, personality, money; who could compete with her?

Scott didn't seem inclined to linger over coffee, and as soon as it was drunk he said abruptly: "Shall we go?" He was silent on the way back to Broomyates, and Drina was glad when they reached the house. She thanked him formally for the meal, and then slipped across to the stable flat where Lois was sprawled in a chair watching a television programme on the set Marc had rented for her from a shop in Canterbridge.

"What's the matter with you?" she enquired when Drina came in. "You don't look as if you'd enjoyed your evening much. I called at the house to have a word with you, but Elfrida said you were dining out with Scott."

"Yes, I stayed at the factory to finish some urgent work for him, and he invited me out for a meal."

"But you didn't enjoy it?"

"It was quite pleasant."

"Then why look so despondent?"

Why indeed? Drina asked herself. It wasn't even as if she liked Scott, so why should Vanessa's arrival on the scene have upset her? She banished all thought of him from her mind, and asked: "Where's Marc?"

Lois yawned. "Working late. He's so wrapped up in this design lark that I hardly see him during the week. It's all very well for him, but doesn't he think I ever want to go out in the evenings?"

"Be patient with him, Lois. I think it gave him a

nasty jolt when he discovered that he couldn't make a living in Ibiza, and then that it was difficult to get a job when he came back to England."

"That's all very well," grumbled Lois, "but he doesn't have to be so deadly serious about everything. He was so gay and lively when we married; such fun to be with. Now he's changed, but I haven't. I'm willing to work, but I want some fun as well."

"Well, Canterbridge isn't exactly Las Vegas, and there's not much opportunity for painting the town red."

"We could have a night out and go dancing," said Lois obstinately. "I'm not prepared to stay cloistered like this indefinitely."

It was on the following Thursday that Drina was working away in the study when she heard the sound of voices, and to her surprise Scott appeared and behind him a familiar figure.

"Don!" she cried. "Where did you spring from?"

He grinned at her. "Scott wrote to my firm to say that his community centre project was going ahead and invited us to submit a design for the new premises, so as soon as I heard about this, I wangled the job of coming down here to survey the site. As I've been rushing round the country ever since the cruise there hasn't been a chance to get in touch with you, so I couldn't pass up this opportunity of seeing you again. How are you, Drina? You look as lovely as ever."

"Thank you. It must be country air which agrees with me."

"When are you going to come up to town for the weekend so that I can take you out? I'm due for some leave shortly, so what about us fixing something up?"

"I'm not sure," began Drina, and then Scott interrupted dryly: "Do you mind if we go out and inspect the site for the centre? I must get back to the office for a meeting at twelve o'clock."

"Of course," said Don smoothly. "See you later, Drina," and the two of them went out.

Drina felt her spirits rise. It had been nice seeing Don again, even if he hadn't made much effort to contact her during the last few weeks. For that matter, she hadn't really expected him to think of her at all. Everyone knew that holiday friendships usually died a quick death, and she had been prepared for this to happen since she didn't want Don to nourish false hopes. All the same, she wasn't averse to a little pleasure, and if he asked her to go out with him she'd accept his invitation.

She drove to the factory to collect Mr. Carlyon as usual, and when she returned with him she discovered that Don had been invited to stay to lunch. He was enthusiastic about the site for the Centre, and told Scott that if his firm were entrusted with the commission they'd do a good job.

"You'll probably want to get more than one estimate," he said, "but I think you'll find ours as favourable as any. We're very keen on keeping our prices competitive, but at the same time, we don't sacrifice good design to cost. This is an attractive site, and you want the landscaping to do justice."

"Yes, I shall get at least two more estimates," said Scott, "but I shan't necessarily choose the cheapest. This project will be expensive, and I want value for money in every way."

"I agree with you."

When lunch was over Mr. Carlyon went to rest, Scott returned to the factory, and Elfrida took herself into the garden.

"Won't you show me round?" Don asked Drina. "I can spare an hour before I have to go back to town."

"If you want to see the garden Miss Carlyon's a much better guide than I am," Drina told him, but he laughed and caught hold of her hand.

"I don't want to see the garden, I want to talk to you. Aren't there any secluded walks round here?"

"I'm supposed to be working," demurred Drina.

"Couldn't you make it up tonight? I shall be gone by three."

"I suppose I could. Come along then, we'll stroll along the lane and through the spinney. I'm told there are masses of bluebells there in the spring."

It was a crisp day for November, with a gleam of sunlight which would soon be gone. Drina led the way down the lane and through the spinney where dead leaves made a sodden carpet.

"How do you like living in the country?" asked Don.

"Very much. I'll be sorry to go back to London when my job ends here."

"How long do you think it will last?"

"It's difficult to say. It depends how quickly Mr. Carlyon completes the book."

Don grimaced. "That might be quite a while, unless the old boy's a fast worker."

Drina laughed. "He's very thorough, and there's a lot of research to be done."

"Don't say that, or you'll leave me without any hope at all. Can't I tempt you with the bright lights of London?"

"I'm afraid not. I don't want to go through the struggle of looking for another flat, not for a while at least."

"But you'll let me take you out for an evening? Couldn't you come up to town and stay the night with a friend? What about the girl you shared the flat with?"

"She's married now, and I don't want to park myself on her so soon. There's only one bedroom in the flat, so it would mean someone sleeping in the sitting-room."

"I see," said Don gloomily. "Oh, well, I'll have to work out something."

He soon cheered up, and as they walked through the spinney and across a field he began to talk buoyantly about his job and how he meant to take advantage of every opportunity.

"I hope we can get the contract for this centre, and I don't see why we shouldn't. I'll see that the specifications are soon drawn up, because it pays to get your tender in as early as possible."

They completed a circle, and came back to the house again. Don looked at his watch.

"Let's stop in the village for a cup of tea before I leave," he suggested.

"I can't go wandering down to the village when I'm supposed to be working," Drina pointed out, "but, if you'd like something before you go, we could pop into the stable flat and ask my sister to make us a pot of tea, or if she isn't there I'll put the kettle on myself."

"The stable flat?"

"Yes. You remember I told you Lois and Marc were here temporarily."

"So you did."

"Lois works in a boutique in Canterbridge, but it's closed on Thursdays."

They mounted the staircase and knocked on the blue front door. Lois answered it, wearing a checked apron over a yellow sweater and brown slacks. Her blonde hair was ruffled, and she looked very delectable as she gazed at them in surprise.

"This is Don Madderley whom I met on the

cruise," said Drina. "He's come down to inspect the site Scott's acquiring for the centre. Don, this is my sister, Lois Chelmsford."

"Come in," invited Lois. "I'll put the kettle on. Drina's mentioned you several times."

"I hope she said flattering things about me."

"I shan't pander to your ego by repeating them," laughed Lois.

When she had drunk a cup of tea, Drina said : "I must fly. Look at the time, and I haven't done a thing this afternoon. Minister to Don, will you, Lois, and see him on his way."

"I will," promised Lois.

"I'll ring you," said Don, "and we'll fix a date for our evening out."

"All right," Drina agreed, and ran back to the house.

She worked steadily until dinner time, and then, when the meal was over, she returned to the stable flat. Marc was there, but after a few minutes' conversation he excused himself and went into the bedroom to work.

"I like your Don," said Lois. "We got on very well together."

"What time did he leave?" enquired Drina.

"I'm not sure. About four, I think."

"He told me he had to start back at three."

"Well, he didn't seem in much of a hurry. He ate several scones and drank three cups of tea. He mentioned that he'd asked you to go out for the evening with him."

"Yes, he did, but it hardly seems worth trailing up to London just for a show or a dance. I'd have to stay the night and I don't want the extra expense of an hotel room."

"Why don't you ask him here for a weekend, and go out to somewhere near at hand?"

Drina stared at her sister. "You mean fix him up at the White Swan in Canterbridge?"

"No, I could put him up here. I could squeeze that folding bed into the boxroom, and I don't suppose he'd mind there not being any other furniture but a chair."

"I don't suppose he would, but the Carlyons might object."

"Why should they? The stable flat's my home, and I can ask whom I like there."

"But what about Marc?"

"What about him?"

"He mightn't care for the idea."

"Why not? Don wouldn't cause him any extra work."

"Well, if you're sure you don't mind," said Drina slowly.

"Of course I don't mind, otherwise I wouldn't have suggested it. I'd only need to give Don breakfast, because you'd be eating out the rest of the time."

Don rang Drina in a couple of days and proposed they should go out together the next Friday evening. She told him of Lois's offer, and he accepted with enthusiasm.

"That's very kind of your sister, and will make things much easier. Where shall we go?"

"I've been told about a country club where we can dine and dance. It's on the far side of Canterbridge, about ten miles away."

"Fine. I'll leave the office early on Friday, and be with you about half past six."

"Lucky you," sighed Lois when Drina told her of the arrangement. "I'll make up a bed for Don, and give him a key so that we needn't wait up for him."

Drina found herself looking forward to the evening.

She enjoyed dancing, and hadn't done any since the cruise. She considered visiting Vanessa's boutique and buying a new dress, but it seemed extravagant when she'd hardly worn her ivory crêpe powdered with tiny gold beads. With that dress, her hair looked best piled high with a false knot of curls on the crown, but when she asked Robert Carlyon if she might have the afternoon off to go to the hairdresser's he refused his permission. She was surprised at this because several times she had worked on into the evening to complete a particular piece of research for him, and her feelings must have been reflected in her face because he said irritably : "What do you want to go dancing with this Madderley fellow for? I thought we'd seen the last of him when the cruise finished. You didn't seem very smitten with him then."

"It's not a question of being smitten," answered Drina, "but I can't shut myself up here, Mr. Carlyon. I need some relaxation at the weekends."

"Yes, yes, of course, but not with him. If you'd only waited a little while...oh, well, go if you must, but you're not to make a habit of it. You can't expect to have every Friday afternoon off to titivate yourself."

Drina bit back a hasty retort, thanked him, and sat down to work, determined not to give him any cause for complaint. She would be chary of asking a favour again, but probably the occasion wouldn't arise. She didn't think Don was the type to persevere with a girl if he weren't making progress, and this evening together could be the first and the last.

On the Friday morning she woke with a sore throat and a headache, but persuaded herself that if she took two aspirins she would soon be all right. She did feel rather better after these and a cup of coffee, and managed to work all morning and go to the hairdresser's in the afternoon. She fell asleep under the dryer and woke with a hot and throbbing head, but by then, it was too late to put Don off. She managed to struggle into her dress and greet him brightly when he arrived, but by the time they reached the Country Club she was already longing for the evening to be over.

"You're looking lovely," said Don admiringly as they reached their table, and insisted on ordering champagne, though Drina protested that it was too expensive.

"Nonsense, it's the first time I've taken you out in England, so we must celebrate, but it won't be the last. Come back to London, Drina. We could have such a good time together this winter."

"I can't come back yet, not until the first draft of the book is finished."

"That's ridiculous; the old boy couldn't force you to stay on. By the way, you didn't tell me your sister was a twin. From the back, you're very much alike, but not so much in the face."

"No, Lois is definitely prettier than I am. When she was modelling she used to look really ravishing, but she hasn't had so much time or money to spend on herself lately."

"She still looks good, you both do," said Don gallantly. "Have some more champagne."

"No more, or else I shall be reeling back to Broomyates, and Scott would definitely disapprove of that."

"So would your boss, I imagine. You know, I wouldn't like to get across him. I'm convinced he could be pretty ruthless if he wanted his own way."

Drina remembered Scott once hinting as much, but she didn't feel inclined to pursue the subject. Instead she said: "Tell me about your job. What have you been doing lately? It must be absorbing travelling up and down the country and meeting all kinds of people."

"It has its lighter side," and Don began to talk amusingly about his experiences.

For a little while, the champagne had stimulated Drina, but now the effect had worn off and she began to feel hot and cold in turn. She concluded that she must have caught a chill, and though she was reluctant to spoil Don's enjoyment, she longed to be tucked up in bed.

"I think we ought to be going," she managed to say, but Don answered immediately: "Oh, not yet, it's still early. Let's have another dance."

"I can't dance any more, I've got a blinding headache," confessed Drina, and Don peered at her.

"You do look rather flushed. Perhaps we had better go."

"I'll be all right after a night's sleep," Drina assured him, and thankfully collected her wrap from the cloak-room.

The headache grew worse on the journey home, and she had to bite her lip hard to prevent herself from betraying how wretched she felt. If only she could get safely to her room she was sure she would feel a great deal better in the morning, so when the car pulled up outside the front door at Broomyates she said hastily: "If you don't mind I'll go straight up to bed, Don. Thank you for a lovely evening."

"I suppose it would be best," he agreed, though he was obviously disappointed at being dismissed so sum-marily. "I'll see you in the morning, then."

He parked his car outside the stable flat, and Drina let herself into the house. Now she had only to cross the hall and climb the stairs, so she took a deep breath and willed herself to make the journey. A wave of faintness came over her, but she conquered it, and was making her unsteady way to the foot of the stairs when Scott came out of the sitting-room. She swallowed convulsively, praying that he wouldn't speak to her, but he came towards her.

"You're back earlier than I expected," he said coolly, and then his eyes took in her pallid face and her unsteady gait. His mouth curled in contempt.

"If your idea of having a good time is to come home in this condition then it doesn't say much for your common sense," he remarked bitingly. "I should have thought Madderley would have taken better care of you than let you drink so much."

"You're mistaken. I've only had one glass of champagne," said Drina weakly, and then she shivered violently and felt the world dissolve about her. Dimly, she was aware that as her legs crumpled beneath her someone who could only be Scott had caught her. Her last conscious thought was that he must be cursing her for all the trouble she was causing, and then she was falling, down, down, down and everything blacked out.

When she came round she was in her own bed, and the room was half dark, lit only by the glow of the electric fire. Her throat was no longer sore and her head was clear, but she felt extraordinarily limp, as if all her strength had drained away. She lay there until presently Elfrida came in and tiptoed to the bedside. When she saw that Drina was awake, she beamed.

"Oh, you're awake at last. I am glad. How do you feel?"

"As if I'd been beaten all over," said Drina feebly. "How long have I been here?"

"Two days. It's Sunday night."

Drina's mind groped back. "And Don?"

"He had to go back to London this afternoon, but he

97

left a message to say that he'd ring tomorrow. He was very upset when he knew you'd collapsed. He said you'd complained of a headache at dinner, and the doctor said you must have picked up a virus that's going about."

"Was that what was wrong? I'm afraid Scott thought I was drunk when I arrived home on Friday night."

"Not when he saw you properly. He called me, and we got you to bed before ringing the doctor. You were running a high temperature yesterday, but you certainly look a lot better tonight."

"I'm sorry to be giving you all this trouble."

"It's no trouble at all. Drink this chicken broth, and then I'll sponge your face and hands. Your sister said she'd be along this evening to sit with you."

Even to drink the broth was an effort, and Drina was glad to sink back on her pillows again. Before long, Lois appeared, and said: "Well, you're a nice one to invite a boy-friend down for the weekend and then fold up on him!"

"I feel dreadfully guilty about that," confessed Drina. "I'm surprised he stayed on. I thought he would have gone home yesterday morning."

"I persuaded him to stay since he would have been at a loose end if he'd returned to London. Marc was working yesterday, so Don and I drove to the coast. We found a little bay which was almost deserted, and though the weather was cold it was fine, so we walked along the sand and afterwards went to a hotel for lunch. It was full of elderly ladies with little dogs, but the food was quite good and we sat for a long time over coffee. Then we dawdled through the country lanes, had a cup of tea, and I arrived back to cook a meal for Marc."

"Didn't he object to your being away all day with Don?"

"Why should he? Although it was Saturday he stayed

at the factory poring over his designs until five o'clock."

"Because he thought you were working at the boutique, I expect. How did you explain your absence to Vanessa?"

"I rang her up and told her I couldn't come in because you were ill. She wasn't very pleased, but I'll make the time up," said Lois airily. "You didn't mind my going out with Don, did you? We made sure first that there was nothing we could do for you, and when there wasn't it seemed a pity to waste the whole day."

"Why should I mind? Don and I are good friends, but there's nothing more to it than that."

"So you said before, but I wondered."

"How are things at the boutique? I must come in and choose a new dress for Christmas."

"Yes, do. We have some things I know you'll like. I've marked down a pale green model which I'm hoping I can get at cost price. Vanessa's certainly got an eye for clothes. I suppose it's living in Italy for so long."

Lois chattered on, and Drina listened, finding it an effort to talk. Finally Lois announced that she must go since there were several things she had to do, and Drina was left to doze. She heard the door open gently and raised her head to see Scott standing at the foot of the bed.

"Oh," she said confusedly. "I thought it must be your aunt."

"She reported that you were feeling better. My grandfather wanted to come along and see you, but he knew that your sister was here, and he thought that perhaps you shouldn't have too many visitors at once. Yes, you certainly look better than you did on Friday night, and I must apologize for what I said to you then. I jumped to the wrong conclusion."

"It doesn't matter, I'm only sorry for all the fuss and trouble I've caused. I should never have gone to the Country Club, but I didn't want to disappoint Don."

"Naturally not," agreed Scott dryly.

"I shall be able to get up tomorrow," went on Drina.

"Try getting out of bed first. You may find that you don't feel as strong as you think you will."

"But I must get up," said Drina resolutely. "There's your grandfather to drive to the factory, to say nothing of the work on the book."

"We can send a car from the factory for him, and it won't matter if the book's neglected for a few days."

Drina blinked at him in surprise. She had expected him to be impatient and irritable with her for holding things up, but instead he was behaving as if he were sorry that she was ill. It was disconcerting, and it left her at a loss for something to say.

Mr. Carlyon came to see her the next morning. She had insisted on getting out of bed to go to the bathroom, and was appalled at her weakness. She might have been in bed for a month instead of only two days. However, when she tried to apologize to her employer he brushed it aside.

"Don't be silly; how could you help falling ill? It happens to all of us, and we must make sure you've really recovered before you start work again. It's a pity the weather isn't good, but you must get out as much as you can."

During the next three days she took several short walks in the garden, but it was too cold to go far on foot. On the Thursday she announced that she was fit enough to start work the next day, but Mr. Carlyon wouldn't hear of it.

"Nonsense," he said, "you must wait until Monday, and in the meantime, you need a little break to take you out of yourself. Scott, you're going over to see that timber firm tomorrow afternoon, aren't you? How about taking Drina with you? She can stroll about while you're discussing business."

"Certainly," answered Scott, "if she'd like to come."

Drina had no alternative but to say she would, though she was aware that it must be the last thing he wanted. However, time dragged heavily when she wasn't allowed to do anything, and by the following afternoon she was longing to get out of the house and welcomed the chance of a trip.

The firm Scott was visiting lay well beyond Canterbridge, and they were soon out in the country.

"Your great-grandfather lived near here as a boy, didn't he?" remarked Drina. "Mr. Carlyon mentioned it one day when he was telling me that originally he'd meant to write his father's biography, but decided he hadn't enough material for that. It's a pity because it would have been interesting to trace the firm right back to its beginning."

"Yes, I'm sorry I never knew the old boy, but he died before I was born. By all accounts he was very like my grandfather, but with even more drive. Funny it should have skipped the third generation entirely."

"You mean your father?"

"And Elfrida. Nice people, both of them, but quite without ambition. My father always seemed a shadowy figure to me, quiet and withdrawn. His hobby was collecting fossils which he kept in display cases in the attic. I was never allowed to touch them. He died when I was eight, from pneumonia. He was out on one of his expeditions, and was caught and drenched in a violent thunderstorm several miles from home."

Scott related this quite casually, but Drina was suddenly overwhelmed with compassion. Poor little boy, losing his mother at six and his father at eight, and brought up by a dominating grandfather. It was a wonder his spirit hadn't been crushed, but casting a sidelong glance at him Drina was aware of the firmness of his mouth and chin. He certainly wasn't without ambition; he had inherited too much determination from his grandfather and great-grandfather for that.

Aloud she said: "Your aunt has a real talent for flower arranging, though. It's a pity she hasn't been able to develop it."

"A great pity, but I'm hoping it isn't too late. She was telling me that you'd suggested holding a Flower Festival in the church at Easter. It's a very good idea, and I don't see why it shouldn't be a success. It's just what Elfrida needs, to believe that she can contribute something valuable to the community."

"Yes," agreed Drina warmly. "Because she doesn't shine domestically she's convinced herself that she's a complete failure, and it's all wrong."

"I'm grateful to you for bolstering up her ego, and I'm determined that this Flower Festival shall be a triumph for her. It's very important that nothing should go wrong."

"Vitally important, and I'll help her all I can."

Scott broke off to say: "The next turning to the right, and we're there. What do you want to do while I'm discussing business? Take a walk as my grandfather suggested? I shall probably be about an hour."

They were on the outskirts of a small country town, and Drina said: "I'd like some exercise. I could stroll into the town, and we could arrange to meet somewhere."

"There's a hotel called the Bridge Arms in the main street. I'll meet you there, and we'll have tea before we start back."

"Right," agreed Drina, and when he stopped the car she climbed out and set off.

There were trees lining the pavement, and as she reached the Bridge Arms, she saw that it was set back with a cobbled square in front of it. On either side were shops, one selling antiques, and Drina peered in the window, then, attracted by a pink and gold lustre jug, she went inside.

The assistant was in conversation with a customer, so Drina picked up the jug, found to her disappointment that it had a crack in it, and turned her attention to a tray of antique jewellery on a side table. There was one piece which particularly attracted her, a square brooch outlined in turquoises and pearls but with a dark oblong in the centre.

The lady who had been admiring the Sheffield plate teapot decided not to buy it, so the assistant moved towards Drina.

"This brooch," said the girl. "Is that a stone in the middle? I can't quite make it out."

The other women picked up the brooch. "No, not a stone, it's a tiny plait of hair. This is a love token, the kind of present a Victorian lover would give his sweetheart. It's pretty, isn't it?"

"Very pretty," agreed Drina. "How much is it?"

"Twenty pounds."

"Oh, that's quite out of my price range, I'm afraid."

"We have one or two cheaper pieces. This gold arrow with the single pearl is fifteen pounds."

"Thank you, but I didn't come in intending to buy a brooch. It happened that the turquoise one attracted me."

Drina left the shop just as Scott's car drew up outside the Bridge Arms. He got out saying : "Have you been buying something interesting?"

"I haven't been buying anything, only admiring a turquoise and pearl brooch which had a plait of hair in the centre. It was very attractive, but too expensive for me. I wonder what the girl looked like who plaited her hair to put in that brooch?"

"I wonder. Let's go in here for a cup of tea. I've talked myself hoarse trying to persuade our timber suppliers to reduce their prices."

"And did you succeed?"

"Partly. I came up a bit, they came down a bit, and in the end we agreed on a figure."

The Bridge Arms provided tea and toasted buns, and the two of them chatted away amiably, more amiably than ever before, Drina realized. For the first time she found herself really enjoying his company, and when he finally glanced at his watch and announced that they had better be moving, she rose to her feet with a reluctance that she wouldn't have believed possible a week ago.

CHAPTER SIX

AT the next community centre committee meeting it was decided that Elfrida should arrange a Flower Festival in the church at Easter while the youth club should lead a sponsored walk on the Bank Holiday. At the same time Vanessa suggested a fancy dress ball to be held in the early part of the year, and this idea was discussed at length.

"What about refreshments?" asked another committee member.

"We could ask one of the restaurants in Canterbridge to supply them," said Vanessa. "I'll arrange for that if you like."

"The Women's Guild have usually catered for any function in the Village Hall," put in the Vicar.

Vanessa smiled at him prettily. "But this won't be the usual 'hop', so we'll need more sophisticated fare than potted meat sandwiches and home-made scones."

The butcher looked indignant, and the Vicar said hastily: "Well, all that can be decided later, when we've fixed on a date. Now, is there any more business?"

The meeting broke up, and Scott saw the committee members to the door. In the hall, Vanessa linked her arm with his and stood with him to say good night to the others, almost as if they were husband and wife. Drina noticed this, and also that Scott didn't seem to object. They all walked back into the drawing-room, and Vanessa said: "What a tribe of stick-in-the-muds! Not one original idea in their heads."

"They haven't your cosmopolitan outlook," said Scott mildly, "but they're very reliable. If they promise to support a thing they do it to the best of their ability."

"And I don't?"

"I didn't imply that."

"I'm sure they're all very worthy, but they're so dull. I like living down here, but I do miss stimulating conversation. You're the only person I can talk to, and you're at the factory all day. I think I'll go up to London to do some Christmas shopping and visit the theatre. Why don't you come too? We could have a good time together."

"At the moment we're too busy at the factory for me to be spared. With Grandfather only going in the mornings there's really no one to take any responsibility if I'm away."

"But your grandfather's never going to be able to do a full day's work again, so hadn't you better start training someone?"

"I'm doing that, but it takes time."

"Oh well, if you won't you won't," sighed Vanessa, "but we could have had such fun."

Scott smiled down at her. "Later on I'll be able to have a break."

"I'll hold you to that."

Drina began to think about Christmas herself. Mr. Carlyon hadn't mentioned giving her any time off, and if he did she had nowhere to go with Lois being up here. Then one evening at dinner he said: "Well, Elfrida, what are your plans for Christmas? I suppose we'll be having some kind of celebration?"

"I was wondering if you'd like to go to a hotel, Father," said Elfrida hesitatingly. "Some of the

London hotels have very gay programmes of festivities."

"I should hate the idea of a hotel," snorted her father. "Christmas ought to be celebrated in one's own home."

"Yes, of course, but Mrs. Braine will expect some time off. Perhaps I could persuade her to take Boxing Day when we could manage with cold stuff."

"You pamper that woman too much, Elfrida. You should make her understand that you're the mistress of the house. Drina, you must invite your sister and her husband for Christmas dinner. The more the merrier."

"Thank you," murmured Drina, and mentioned the proposal to Lois.

"I expect you'd rather celebrate on your own," she suggested, but Lois shook her head.

"Oh no, it will be more fun to be in a party. I wasn't looking forward to cooking a chicken just for Marc and myself."

Christmas crept nearer, and Drina took an afternoon off to shop for presents in Canterbridge. For Marc she bought a bottle of whisky, a book on flower arranging for Elfrida and the latest biography for Mr. Carlyon, then she walked along to the boutique to see what Vanessa had in stock.

It was only the second time she had trodden its French grey carpet, and she was hoping that Vanessa would be engaged with another customer, but her luck was out. It was Lois who was coping with a plump woman who was convinced she could squeeze into a size fourteen, and Vanessa who came forward to greet Drina.

"Hallo," she said casually. "What can we do for you?"

"I'm looking for a dress to wear on Christmas Day in the evening," answered Drina. She regarded the simple black wool dress trimmed with rows of black ciré ribbon which Vanessa was wearing and added: "Something rather like the one you have on."

"I bought this in Rome, it's a Terraza model," said Vanessa sweetly. "But thank you for the compliment. Let's see what we have which would fit you. Size sixteen?"

"Twelve," answered Drina evenly.

Vanessa raised her eyebrows. "Really? You give the impression of having big bones."

She walked to the back of the showroom, and ran her hands along the rack. "What about this?"

This was a crêpe in a fashionable but ugly shade of dark red. Drina shook her head.

"I know that shade's all the rage, but I don't like it. Tawny shades suit me. Have you anything in a clear amber?"

"I don't think so. Tan, perhaps. There's this."

Vanessa held up a tan and black dress, and Drina considered it.

"Yes, that a possible."

"And this green is your size."

It was a dull green in a soft clinging material and Drina regarded it dubiously, then reflected that it might look better on than in the hand.

"I'll try these two."

In the small cubicle with its elegant lilac and silver stripes she tried on both the dresses. The green she rejected immediately, but the tan fitted her well, and she turned this way and that to see the full effect in the long mirrors. The trouble was that the dress didn't do anything for her. It was adequate but no more, and while she was trying to make up her mind whether she would do better somewhere else Lois came into the cubicle.

"Oh, not that," she said at once, "it isn't you."

Vanessa stood in the doorway, and regarded Drina appraisingly.

"It's a very good fit; it wouldn't require any alteration."

Lois wrinkled her brow. "It would be all right for an office, but not for a Christmas party."

"Party?" echoed Vanessa smoothly. "How exciting."

"It isn't a party, only a family dinner," said Drina hastily.

"Nevertheless, you want to look your best," said Lois. "I'll bet Mr. Carlyon's kissed a few girls under the mistletoe in his time. He has that look in his eye."

"So the Carlyons are going to celebrate Christmas at home? How nice. I thought they might be going away."

"The hollyberry dress," said Lois suddenly. "It's much more your type, Drina."

"Oh, I hardly think—" began Vanessa, but Lois had darted away and she came back in a moment with a drift of scarlet over her arm.

"Try this," she said triumphantly, and shook it out. Drina hesitated.

"You don't think it's too bright?"

"No, I don't," said Lois emphatically, and swooped forward to drop the soft folds of chiffon over her sister's head.

Drina let out her breath. Lois was right, unbelievably right. The brilliant colour was the perfect foil for her hair, and if she had any doubts they would have been resolved by the flash of annoyance she saw in Vanessa's eyes.

The other woman said: "Yes, it's quite becoming, but it's a colour you'd soon tire of. Something not quite so conspicuous would be more practical."

"Who wants to be practical?" shrugged Lois. "Far better to wear a dress which does something for you."

"Yes," agreed Drina. "I'll take it."

It cost more than she'd intended to pay, but she didn't regret her extravagance. Lois offered to bring the dress home with her that evening so that her sister needn't be encumbered with the box while she was doing the rest of her shopping, and Drina left the shop. She still had presents to buy for Lois herself, and for Scott. It was a problem to decide what to get him as she didn't know his tastes in books sufficiently well to choose for him, and a token seemed rather unenterprising. However, she was on the point of buying one in desperation when she saw some square chunky cuff-links which she thought might suit him, and settled for those. A bra and pants set with a matching half slip in coffee-coloured nylon and lace for Lois completed her purchases, and then she returned to Broomyates.

"This dress is absolutely you," declared Lois when she handed it in on her way home. "I can't think why Vanessa didn't show it to you."

I can, Drina told herself. She can't bear the thought of competition, even from someone as insignificant as me. She hates me, but I wonder why. Scott would never look twice at me under any circumstances.

The next day, Lois reported that Vanessa was going up to London for a couple of days.

"She says she really can't do her Christmas shopping in Canterbridge, there's absolutely no choice of goods, so she'll travel up to London tomorrow and come back on Friday night, which means that I shall be in charge on Friday. In return she's not opening the shop on Saturday, so I shall have a free weekend."

"Good, that means you'll be able to come to the woods. Elfrida and I are going to gather holly and pine cones to use as Christmas decorations. We're starting directly after lunch."

So on Saturday Elfrida donned an ancient tweed coat, and armed herself with a large basket, after directing Drina to do the same.

"Where are you going?" asked Scott, coming into the hall as they were setting out.

"To the woods to gather holly," answered his aunt. "Do you remember how we used to do it when you were a little boy? I'm afraid I haven't bothered for several years, but I thought it would be fun to make a special effort this year."

"Why not?" he said. "Wait a moment and I'll join you. I could do with some exercise."

Lois was waiting at the gate, and the four of them walked through the village and along the lane which led to the woods. Vanessa's house lay half way along it, and as they passed her garden gate, she called to them and came running down the drive. There was no old tweed coat for her, or an ancient anorak like Drina's, but a fur-lined suède coat and boots, together with a white fox hood which made her look like the Snow Queen.

"May I come too?" she cried. "You can only be going to one place, carrying sticks and baskets. This is really like old times, Scott, when we were children and used to come back loaded with holly. The best bits with berries on were always out of my reach, so you used to have to pull them down for me."

He smiled. "Yes, and got myself well scratched in the process."

When they reached the woods, Elfrida was transformed. She decided that Scott was to gather holly, and the rest of them were to look for pine cones, trails of ivy, and twigs which could be covered with gold and silver paint. Vanessa attached herself to Scott, and she and he wandered off together, her laughter echoing through the trees every now and then.

At last, loaded with booty, they set off back to Broomyates. Vanessa suggested that they stop at her house first for a drink, but Elfrida said that her father would be waiting for his tea as Mrs. Braine was off duty in the afternoons. They walked along in the frosty twilight, and Vanessa said enthusiastically: "I have enjoyed my afternoon. It takes me right back to the Christmases of my childhood. I remember when I could hardly wait for Christmas Day, and the presents to be taken off the tree. I always wanted the fairy doll off the top to keep, but it had to be put away to be used another year."

"I remember the year when I wanted a bicycle and I got a train set instead," said Scott reminiscently.

"You never cared much for trains," said Elfrida. "I think your father really bought it so that he could manipulate it himself."

"While I was in London, I contemplated booking into a hotel for the holiday," remarked Vanessa, "but when it came to the point I couldn't do it. Christmas is such a family time, isn't it, though heaven knows I've no one to share it with."

The hint was blatant, and Elfrida looked uncomfortable.

"We shan't be doing anything exciting," she mumbled, "but if you'll be alone we'd be happy for you to join us, wouldn't we, Scott?"

"Of course," he agreed.

"I'd love to come," cried Vanessa, radiant now that she had achieved what she had been angling for, and she looked up at Scott with her most beguiling air. He gazed down at her indulgently, and Drina wondered if Vanessa ever failed to get what she wanted.

The day before Christmas Eve was given up to decorating the hall and the drawing-room, and here Elfrida came into her own. There were miniature trees hung with baubles in each room, and she achieved a wonderful Grinling Gibbons effect with trails of silvered ivy and gilded pine cones. Flushed with triumph, she created for the dining-room table a centrepiece of fruit and flowers which resembled a Dutch still life, and when Drina congratulated her on it she said deprecatingly: "Isn't it strange, I can manage this without effort, and yet I can't bake an edible cake."

"You don't need to, with a gift like yours."

It was on the morning of Christmas Eve that disaster struck. Elfrida went to the kitchen as usual after breakfast, then rushed back into the dining-room to break the news that Mrs. Braine had announced that she wanted to spend Christmas Day with her sister in Fulham.

"If only she'd mentioned it before," cried Elfrida, wringing her hands, "but it's too late to ask anyone else to cook the Christmas dinner, and what am I to do with the turkey? I've never roasted one in my life!"

"One of the daily women must come in," said her father irritably. "Offer her double wages."

"It wouldn't be any use; they all want to be with

their families on Christmas Day. Originally, Mrs. Braine agreed to take the New Year off instead of Christmas, but now she says she's had a letter to say that her sister isn't well and wants to see her."

"Don't worry, Lois and I will cope," said Drina reassuringly. "I've cooked a chicken several times, and the same rules apply to a turkey."

"And I'm a dab hand at peeling potatoes," said Scott cheerfully.

"Well, if you're sure—" Elfrida looked pathetically grateful at the prospect of having all the responsibility taken from her shoulders. "What's the first thing to do?"

"Stuff the bird," said Drina, glad now of the lessons her aunt, who was a capable housewife, had given her. "When I've taken Mr. Carlyon to the factory, I'll come into the kitchen and look at it."

After she had dropped Mr. Carlyon, she drove into Canterbridge and bought a cookery book to refresh her memory. She was determined that Vanessa shouldn't find any cause to criticize the food which was put in front of her, and when she returned to Broomyates she set about stuffing the turkey. At least Mrs. Braine kept a good store cupboard, and Drina discovered everything there which was needed. The pudding was neatly tied up in its basin, and there were several jars of mincemeat, so Drina baked a batch of mince-pies. As Scott didn't come home for lunch she made omelettes for Elfrida, Mr. Carlyon and herself, then cooked the loin of lamb which was in the fridge for dinner that evening.

After dinner, she went across to the stable flat to explain the situation to Lois.

"Now's the time to trot out your favourite Spanish recipe," she said. "Didn't you pick up any ideas from that restaurant in Ibiza? Mrs. Braine isn't returning until the day after Boxing Day, so there's plenty of scope for your talents."

Lois giggled. "I might manage a dish of paella. Steven used to put a bit of everything in it, but the result was very tasty."

"I don't think that would appeal to Mr. Carlyon. He's strictly a roast-and-two-vegetables man, and regards everything else with suspicion."

"Then I'm not much use to him. Marc and I live mainly out of tins and packets, with the odd steak on the side when it's not too expensive."

"But Lois and I will come and help out," volunteered Marc. "We can prepare the vegetables, and help with any other chores."

"Scott's offered to peel potatoes," said Drina.

Lois raised her eyebrows. "Has he indeed? You're honoured."

Drina was up early the next morning to get on with breakfast. She pulled on slacks and a sweater and crept into the kitchen to make herself a pot of tea, but to her surprise, as she was pouring out a cup Scott appeared.

"Any for me?" he asked, and she answered: "Plenty," as she reached for another cup and saucer.

"Look," he said, "there's no need for you to slave in the kitchen all day. Even at this short notice I think I could manage to book a table at the White Swan for dinner, and we could all go along there."

Drina shook her head. "Oh no. It would be a pity to waste the turkey, and your grandfather doesn't really want to go to a hotel on Christmas Day."

"He'd see reason if I put it to him."

"There's no need for that. I'll enjoy doing it."

Scott looked at her rather oddly, she thought, and

then said: "Well, if you're sure. What time do you propose to have this meal?"

"About half past seven as usual. According to its weight, the bird ought to go into the oven around three o'clock."

After breakfast they all went to church, and Elfrida provided a scratch lunch of soup and sandwiches. At three o'clock Drina put the turkey into the oven, and the kitchen was soon full of the succulent smell of roasting bird. Scott peeled the potatoes, Lois and Marc prepared the other vegetables and Elfrida set the long dining table. Drina made the brandy butter for the pudding, put the rest of the meal on to cook, and then went to change into the hollyberry dress. She hadn't much time to spend on making up her face, but that didn't really matter, she reflected ruefully, because Vanessa would outshine her, whatever trouble she took.

At seven, when everything was reaching the final stage, Vanessa arrived in a coat and cap of honey-coloured mink, her arms full of parcels.

"I'm so looking forward to this," she cried. "It's years since I spent a family Christmas. Rico always wanted to entertain his friends in hotels. Where shall I put these?"

"Under the tree," said Elfrida. "We aren't opening our presents until after dinner."

The mink coat came off to reveal a fitted dress of honey-coloured velvet which subtly emphasized every curve, and the long topaz and diamond earrings which Vanessa was wearing glittered every time she moved her head. Drina, swathing her dress in an overall while she dished up, had to admit that she had never seen Vanessa looking lovelier, and to subdue a pang of envy. Lois helped to pile the various dishes on to a big heated hostess trolley, and soon Robert Carlyon was carving the turkey while Scott poured the champagne.

"Scott, you angel, you knew this was my favourite," said Vanessa as she raised her glass.

"I thought it would put all of us in the right frame of mind to enjoy the evening," answered Scott, and Vanessa countered meaningly: "It will."

When the meal was over they trooped to the drawing-room where the parcels were piled round the Christmas tree in the window. Lois was looking very pretty in turquoise, and Drina noticed Marc's hand on her arm, and the way his eyes kindled when they rested on his wife.

"Are you going to play Santa Claus, Father, and hand out the presents?" said Elfrida, who was flushed and shiny-nosed in an unbecoming dress of coffee-coloured lace.

"I suppose so," he answered resignedly, "though it seems rather ridiculous considering there isn't a child among us."

He began to distribute the parcels, and Drina found herself with an envelope containing a five-pound note from him, a silk scarf from Vanessa, perfume from Lois and Marc, and two more presents. One proved to be a vanity case from Elfrida, and then Drina turned to the other.

"Open it quickly," cried Vanessa gaily. "It must be from Scott, there's no one else left."

Drina was aware of this too, and wished she could have opened the gift in the privacy of her own room. She tore off the gold and white striped paper to reveal a faded blue morocco case and inside this the turquoise and pearl brooch with the tiny plait of hair inside.

"Oh, Scott," she breathed, "thank you, thank you so much!"

"That's pretty," said Mr. Carlyon approvingly. "Better than all your modern trinkets, and it's exactly your style, Drina."

Drina saw Vanessa's hand clench over the gold lighter Scott had given her, and the look she shot Mr. Carlyon was one of pure hatred. Then in an instant it had vanished, and she was laughing.

"It's certainly very pretty, but I wouldn't change it for my present. I don't think I want to go back to Victorian days, I'm enjoying myself too much in the present." She turned to Scott. "What shall we do now? Can't we put on the record player and dance? Don't you remember how we used to practise in the hall with the rugs rolled up?"

"There's a stack of records here," said Scott. "Choose what you want."

"What a pity your boy-friend isn't here, Drina," sympathized Vanessa. "As it is, we're a man short, but I expect we'll manage."

"Well, I shall go to the study if you intend to play that rackety music," said Mr. Carlyon. "What about you, Elfrida? I don't suppose you want your ears assailed."

His daughter smiled apologetically. "No, I don't, so I'll say good night too. I'm going to have a blissful evening with the book you gave me, Drina. I can't wait to try out some of its suggestions."

Scott rolled up the rugs in the hall and brought in the record player while Vanessa began sorting through a pile of records, eventually holding one up.

"Scott, do you remember this? The band played it the very first time you took me to a dance. Let's try it out now for old times' sake."

The insistent rhythm of the music beat out, and she floated into his arms. Drina stood back against the wall, and a queer little pang shot through her as they circled the hall together, Vanessa looking up at Scott with a caressing smile while his head bent to hers.

After that they all danced in turn, and the two men divided their attention between the three women. Marc was an expert dancer, and when he and Lois partnered each other they were worth watching. Drina felt stiff with Scott, aware that Vanessa's eyes were on them all the time, and she longed for the evening to be over. Presently they all paused for drinks, and Lois said: "I don't know about the rest of you, but I'd love some coffee."

"So would I," said Drina quickly. "We'll go and make some," and she followed her sister to the kitchen.

"It is a pity that Don isn't here," remarked Lois. "Didn't you think of inviting him?"

"I could hardly do that unless Elfrida had suggested it."

"I wonder that she didn't."

"He probably had plans of his own, anyway, and wouldn't have been able to come."

When the coffee was ready, they wheeled it into the drawing-room, and Drina carried a tray into the study.

Elfrida said: "Oh, coffee, how nice! When you've drunk yours, Father, don't you think you ought to go to bed? You're looking tired."

"Yes, perhaps I will. Christmas isn't the same. All that caterwauling music: it's only fit for savages to dance to."

"Let me teach you the cha-cha-cha," said Drina mischievously. "I'm sure you'd soon pick it up."

"Get along with you," he retorted. "I suppose I'd better come and say good night, it's only polite."

He followed her into the drawing-room where Vanessa was sitting on a sofa, her head tilted back as she talked to Scott who was perched on the arm behind her.

"Good night," said Robert Carlyon abruptly. "I'm going to bed," and Vanessa cried : "Not yet, surely?"

Then she rose gracefully to her feet. "If you will stand there, Mr. Carylon, then you can't expect people not to take advantage of it."

She crossed the room, put her hands on his shoulders and kissed his cheek, and it wasn't until then that Drina realized he was positioned under a ball made of mistletoe threaded with silver ribbon.

"If you're reduced to kissing me," he said dryly, "then these two young men haven't been making the most of their opportunities."

"They're so slow," and Vanessa raised inviting eyes to Scott.

There was nothing slow about his reaction. In two long strides he reached Vanessa and swept her into his arms where she clung, her lovely mouth pressed eagerly to his.

"Fair shares for all," said Scott smoothly as he released her and seized Lois who was nearest to him, kissing her as heartily.

"Now Drina," said Mr. Carlyon, and the girl felt her cheeks flush as Scott reached her in turn. His kiss didn't mean anything to her, she told herself, it couldn't. What was a kiss under the mistletoe at Christmas? But all the same she was undeniably shaken when his mouth came down on hers. His lips were cool, hard, insistent, and her blood began to beat with a dangerous rhythm. It was agony, it was ecstasy, and though she'd been kissed by several men in her time this was like nothing she'd experienced before. Her eyes were tightly closed, and when she opened them it was to see Scott looking down at her with an unfathomable expression on his face. Then, the next second, he had released her, and Marc was saying : "My turn now, I think."

"Let's dance again," cried Vanessa, but Drina excused herself, knowing that she couldn't bear to circle the room in Scott's arms after that kiss.

"I expect you're feeling tired," said Marc sympathetically. "Don't forget you were busy all the afternoon with preparations for the meal, and very good it was too."

"I had plenty of help," protested Drina, "and there was nothing very difficult about what I did."

But when the others were leaving Scott echoed Marc's words as he closed the front door behind his guests.

"Thank you for making it such a pleasant Christmas Day," he said when he had seen Vanessa to her car.

"I enjoyed what I did," Drina assured him. "It's a long time since I enjoyed a Christmas Day so much either. Good night."

"Good night," he answered, but though she acknowledged her weariness, when she reached her room she didn't undress immediately. Instead she sat on the edge of the bed, and found herself reliving the memory of that kiss. Then she scolded herself inwardly for dwelling on something which had no significance at all, and unzipped her dress.

No one seemed very energetic on Boxing Day, and Scott disappeared after lunch. Drina wondered if he had gone to see Vanessa, and went for a walk herself, coming back to find Mr. Carlyon alone in the sitting-room.

"Would you like a cup of tea?" she asked, "or would you rather wait for Miss Carlyon?"

"No, we'll have it cosily by the fire, just the two of us," he answered. "Elfrida's gone down to the village to see that new friend of hers, Joan Someone-or-other, and I told her not to hurry back."

Drina went to put on the kettle and set out the trolley with toasted scones and cake.

"This is very nice," commented Mr. Carlyon as she poured out the tea. "You have a gift for making a room seem comfortable and lived in; you're a born home-maker, Drina. I sensed it as soon as I met you. My wife was the same, but Scott's mother was quite different. I shall never understand why my son wanted to marry her, but the less said about that the better."

"Thank you for the compliment," said Drina, rather embarrassed at this praise.

"Yes," went on Mr. Carlyon, "look at the way you cooked that turkey yesterday. It was almost a professional job. My instinct didn't play me false when we met on that ship, and I don't think you've regretted coming here, have you?"

"No, of course not. I've been very happy."

"Scott may find it difficult to reveal his emotions, but he's mellowing towards you, I can tell that. My wife died before he was born, and his own mother deserted him, so apart from Elfrida he didn't have much chance to experience a woman's softening influence. I think that was why he took such a toss over Vanessa, but I was right to put a stop to that affair. She wasn't the wife for him then, and she isn't now. You're much more his type."

A dreadful suspicion crept over Drina. She must be mistaken. It wasn't possible that Mr. Carlyon had deliberately manoeuvred Scott and herself together, had in fact planned for them to marry each other. Yet she couldn't help remembering that day in Madeira how the old man had insisted that she and Scott should go down in the toboggan together, and how he had begged her to take the job here at Broomyates.

She stammered: "But you can't think ... I mean, Scott's never shown the slightest interest in me."

"He's very reserved," said Mr. Carlyon, "but his feelings are there all right, even if they are hidden. That's why I didn't want you to become discouraged."

"I don't understand," said Drina numbly. "I'd no idea that my coming here was all part of a plot. I thought that you genuinely needed me to help with the book."

Mr. Carlyon looked at her benignly. "Certainly I do. I'm deeply serious about writing the book, but there's never any harm in killing two birds with one stone. It was my good fortune to find a competent secretary who was also an attractive and charming girl. If you'd been plain and worthy I'd have hesitated before engaging you, but fortunately I wasn't faced with that dilemma."

"But—" began Drina, only to stop as Elfrida appeared quite out of breath.

"Sorry, Father, I didn't notice the time. Oh, Drina, you've given him some tea. Thank you so much. Joan and I were discussing the Flower Festival. She's as interested in flower arranging as I am, and when she was teaching in school in Chadcaster she helped to arrange an Easter display in the Cathedral. Also she knows where we can borrow containers, pedestal vases and so on. We shall have to try them out at a dress rehearsal some time before the actual event so that we can get an idea of the amount of decoration needed. Is there any tea left in the pot?"

"A little, but it will be cold by now. I'll make some fresh."

"I'll do it," said Elfrida.

"No, it won't take me a moment."

Drina seized the pot and escaped to the kitchen, thankful to be by herself for a few moments. Her thoughts were whirling chaotically in her head, and she didn't know how she was going to face Scott. She had a dreadful feeling that this might have happened before, that she wasn't the first girl his grandfather had tried to foist on to him. Now she could understand his deep suspicion when they first met.

What humiliated her above everything was his belief that she had been a party to the scheme. It was understandable perhaps, but the fact that he was convinced she was that kind of girl made her writhe. She would have liked to take the next train back to London so that she never need see him again. And yet she didn't want to leave Broomyates. What was she to do?

She made the tea and took it back to the sitting-room, but she scarcely heard a word of what Elfrida was saying. It was a relief that Scott didn't come in until immediately before dinner because it gave her the chance to pull herself together, but as soon as the meal was over she made an excuse and disappeared to her room.

It was an impulse she regretted because she couldn't stay there all evening, and she would have to face Scott sooner or later. She made up her face again, and then took a deep breath before walking downstairs. She would put the whole business out of her mind. If she continued to treat Scott with cool friendliness, he would soon realize that he had nothing to fear from her.

Then, just as she reached the hall, he came out of the study, and her good resolutions were shattered in an instant. She stopped short in dismay, and she saw his eyes narrow.

"What's the matter? You look as if I were the last person you expected to see."

"No...that is...." stammered Drina, desperately trying to regain her poise. "Your grandfather...."

"Has he been talking to you? Come in here for a moment," and grasping her wrist, Scott whisked her into the study.

"Now," he demanded, "what did he say to you to put you in such a flurry?"

Drina swallowed hard. "He admitted that he'd deliberately thrown you and me together on the ship, and that he asked me to come here because he thought I was the right type of girl for you."

"I knew that from the first," said Scott calmly.

"And you believed that I was aware of it too, that I was a party to the scheme?"

"Yes, I did. Grandfather isn't very subtle, and he's made no secret of the fact that he wants me to marry. You appeared to fall in with his ideas very prettily, and it seemed likely that you had an eye to the main chance, so I didn't feel disposed to let you get away with it. I shall marry whom I please, and when I please, whether it suits my grandfather or not."

"I hadn't the faintest idea of what he was planning. It was stupid of me not to suspect anything, but—"

"But he was a charming old gentleman and you never dreamed that he had an ulterior motive. All right, I believe you now. If it's any comfort to you, I came to the conclusion some time ago that I'd been mistaken, that you were as much a victim as I was."

"I should hope so," said Drina indignantly. "I don't relish being taken for a harpy, and I've no intention of marrying anybody until I fall in love."

Scott grinned. "Then we're both of the same mind, and none of Grandfather's tricks will have any effect. Is everything straightened out now?"

"Yes," said Drina.

As she smiled up at him she felt relaxed and at ease. She had never thought it would matter to her whether or not Scott believed the worst of her, but all at once it seemed important that he didn't despise her, even if he were going to marry Vanessa.

CHAPTER SEVEN

DRINA had heard only briefly from Don since the weekend he had spent down at Broomyates. There had been a note scribbled in his Christmas card to the effect that he was away in the North of England, drafting the blueprint for a new City Hall, but no indication of when he would return to London, so that she was surprised when Lois mentioned having heard from him.

"I thought he'd deserted us completely," said Drina. "Where is he now?"

"Still in the North," said Lois, "but he hopes to be back in London in a fortnight. Were you considering asking him to the fancy dress ball?"

"I hadn't intended to. I didn't think it would appeal to him."

"Why not? It should be quite good fun, and he could stay the night at the flat again."

"Do you really think he'd enjoy the ball?" queried Drina dubiously. "I think it's going to be very much of a one-man band with Vanessa playing the lead."

"Well, obviously she'll be the star turn," agreed Lois, "but that needn't affect us."

After some argument on the part of the committee it had at last been decided that a fancy dress ball should be held in aid of the fund with Vanessa as its organizer. In practice most of the work had been delegated to Drina, and the girl found herself dashing in and out of Canterbridge comparing estimates from the various catering establishments who had been approached about supplying the refreshments. Vanessa appeared to be wholly engrossed in planning her costume for the affair, and had told Lois that she intended to go as Mary Queen of Scots.

Drina finally decided that Countryside Caterers offered the most advantageous terms, but couldn't give them a definite order without Vanessa's approval, so she called at the boutique to consult the other woman.

"Oh, engage them if you think they sound the best proposition," said Vanessa indifferently, "though I don't suppose their food will be particularly inspired. I think I'll import my own supply of smoked salmon for the occasion. I can't stand those sausage rolls and massive ham sandwiches that the villagers dote on. I expect your friend will be coming down for the ball, won't he?"

"I haven't asked him yet."

"It would be a pity not to. You don't want to find yourself without a partner, and there's no eligible unattached male in the village."

"Oh, Don will come," broke in Lois, "though I'm pretty sure he won't wear fancy dress. I can't even persuade Marc into it."

Vanessa frowned. "After all the trouble we're going to the men ought to co-operate. Since I'm going to be Mary Queen of Scots I'm hoping that Scott will partner me as Bothwell. He has exactly the figure for Elizabethan doublet and hose."

"I haven't heard him mention the ball," said Drina.

"He'll certainly be going," answered Vanessa confidently. "What costume have you decided on?"

"I haven't really thought about it yet. It will have to be something simple. I don't want to go to a lot of expense."

That evening she walked across to the stable flat

and said to Lois: "I suppose we'll have to make some kind of an effort for this ball. Do you think we could capitalize on the fact that we're twins? What famous pairs have there been in fiction? I can only think of Tweedledum and Tweedledee, and they would hardly suit our purpose."

"Hardly. I know, we'll be 'the Heavenly Twins'. The last time I was in Canterbridge market I saw a lot of cheap pale blue nylon which we could make up into draped Grecian dresses. They're easy, because they only need to hang in folds and be caught up on one shoulder. We could cross the bodices with silver ribbons and pile our hair high with a matching ribbon tied round a topknot. We both possess a pair of silver sandals, so we needn't spend much at all."

"What a clever idea! We'll try it."

For the next fortnight Vanessa was constantly in and out of Broomyates. Scott had agreed to go to the ball, but had flatly refused to dress up as Bothwell or any other Elizabethan gallant.

"But you'd look so handsome," declared Vanessa cajolingly, "and we ought to go as a pair. If you'd agree to being Nelson I'd change to Lady Hamilton."

"Not for you or anyone else. Sorry, Vanessa, but I can't play the part. Believe me, you'll look far more effective on your own."

Vanessa made an unsuccessful attempt to swallow her chagrin.

"If you won't you won't, but I think it's a great pity. We can't expect other people to take a lot of trouble to make the ball a success if we won't put ourselves out."

"I don't think my not turning up as Nelson is going to sabotage the affair," said Scott good-humouredly. "Drina tells me that the tickets have sold very well."

"And she's the one who's done all the work," said Robert Carlyon pointedly.

He usually took care to avoid Vanessa if it were possible, but he had emerged from his study while she was talking and now was standing with a book in his hand and a sardonic expression on his face. Vanessa's lips tightened.

"I think I've done my share towards the cause," she said sharply. "I've given the ball a lot of publicity in Canterbridge, otherwise the tickets wouldn't have sold at all."

Scott looked at her in surprise. "I don't think any one of us has been slacking. We're all making a contribution directly or indirectly."

He picked up a sheaf of papers and went out. Vanessa bit her lip, and then recovered her poise.

"It's silly of me to be so edgy, but I'm very anxious for the whole thing to be a success. It's a cause very dear to my heart."

Drina hadn't heard from Don, and she kept reminding herself to ring him about the ball, and then forgetting. Lois had bought the nylon she had seen in Canterbridge market, and between them she and Drina had made two dresses. The material was easy to drape in graceful folds, and Drina was surprised to see how effective it looked when the bodices were crossed with silver ribbon. Over at the stable flat she was adding the finishing touches to her own dress when Marc came in and said: "That's a really attractive colour. Wait until Don sees you in it, Drina."

"If he does," answered Drina. "He may not be able to come to the ball. I—"

"But I understood that he was definitely coming," said Marc with a puzzled frown. "I'm sure Lois said so."

Now it was Drina's turn to look puzzled. "Lois?" she echoed, and her sister broke in quickly with : "Of course he's coming, Drina. You know he was only teasing you."

She directed an appealing look at her twin, and Drina subsided with a vague : "I suppose you're right," determining to tackle Lois about what was going on as soon as she had the opportunity.

This came when her sister announced that they had run out of beer, and Marc decided to go down to the pub for a couple of bottles. As soon as he'd left the flat, Drina said meaningly : "What was all that about Don coming to the ball? I meant to invite him, but I've never got round to it."

"No, but I have," said Lois airily. "He said he'd be delighted to come."

"But why tell Marc I'd asked Don?"

"Because Marc's so ridiculously jealous. You've no idea what it was like in Ibiza. If a Spaniard so much as glanced at me he went up in the air. Don merely gave a friendly ring to ask me how I was, and I mentioned the ball to him since you hadn't had the opportunity to do it. I suppose Marc got the impression that you'd spoken to Don, not me, and since it didn't matter either way I didn't disillusion him."

"I see," said Drina.

It was a very glib explanation, but it didn't ring true. Marc wasn't the type of man to get a wrong impression unless one had been deliberately foisted on him, and Drina experienced a pang of foreboding. Surely there was nothing between Lois and Don? Her sister couldn't be so foolish as to risk her marriage for the sake of a brief affair, but Lois had always lived for the moment and in spite of her work at the boutique she still found Lindisthorpe dull.

"Lois," she began uncertainly, "you wouldn't do anything silly, would you? I mean—"

Her sister stared back at her defiantly. "Oh, don't be so stuffy! You're only the same age as I am, but sometimes you act as if you were ninety. I want a little fun, but these days Marc thinks about nothing but his wretched designs. The fact that I'm bored here and want to go back to London doesn't weigh with him. Don makes me laugh, that's all there is to it."

"You were glad enough to come down here when Marc was finding it impossible to get a job."

Lois shrugged her shoulders pettishly. "I know I was, but I thought it would only be a temporary measure, and that we'd soon be back in London. Unfortunately, Marc likes this place, and I hadn't bargained for that."

"But you could—" began Drina, and then stopped as Marc returned with the beer. During the rest of the evening there wasn't another opportunity for her to be private with Lois, and she had to go back to Broomyates in the unhappy knowledge that Lois was dissatisfied and ripe for mischief.

The next day a large parcel arrived at the boutique which Lois guessed was Vanessa's costume for the Fancy Dress Ball. She was right. Vanessa unpacked it, and then couldn't resist parading in it for the benefit of her assistant. She certainly looked beautiful. The black velvet dress with its tight, low-cut bodice looped with pearls and full skirt was the perfect foil for her red-gold hair and white skin. Lois's admiration was genuine.

Vanessa regarded herself in the mirror with a little smile of satisfaction, and said: "Yes, I don't think I could have chosen better. What did you say you were going to wear, Lois? Pale blue nylon?"

"Yes. Drina and I are going as 'the Heavenly Twins', wearing identical costumes."

"It sounds quite original. Has your sister's boy-friend decided to come down for the ball?"

"Don?" Now it was Lois's turn to wear a smile of satisfaction. "Oh yes, he'll be there."

Vanessa regarded her shrewdly. "Is there any sign of an engagement?"

"I don't think so. They're just good friends."

"In fact, he's attracted to you, isn't he?" said Vanessa softly. "What does your husband think about that?"

"Oh, he doesn't—You're quite mistaken," said Lois quickly.

"I don't think I am, but don't worry, I shan't give anything away. Have some fun while you can. You're old soon enough."

Lois giggled. "That's my motto too."

The following morning, Mr. Carlyon didn't come down to breakfast, and Elfrida reported that he had a slight cold.

"I don't think it's anything very much," she said, "but with his tendency to bronchitis it pays to take care. Naturally, if he grows worse I shall send for the doctor, and I shan't go along to see Joan tonight as I'd arranged."

"There's no need for you to sacrifice your evening," said Drina. "I shall be staying in, and if Mr. Carlyon's condition deteriorated I could ring the doctor immediately."

"But it wouldn't be fair to put the responsibility on to you," began Elfrida, whereupon Scott interrupted her with : "There's no question of that. I'm not going out this evening, so I shall be at hand."

"I thought you'd probably be calling on Vanessa," said his aunt.

Scott shook his head. "No, for once I intend to relax at home. I want to watch a documentary on the television."

"The wildlife programme?" queried Drina. "It should be very interesting. I've enjoyed the series so far."

"Unfortunately I've missed most of it, but since I've nothing on hand tonight I thought I'd stay in to view. What about watching with me?"

"Thank you, I'd like that," accepted Drina.

After dinner she helped Elfrida to load the dishes into the dishwasher, and then went back to the sitting-room where Scott was sprawled in a chair with his long legs stretched out in front of the fire.

"Let's make ourselves comfortable with a drink before the programme starts," he suggested. "What will you have? Sherry, gin and tonic, or whisky?"

Drina chose sherry, and he poured it out together with a whisky for himself. As he stooped to pass her the glass, Drina noticed how long his eyelashes were, and suddenly it was as though every nerve in her body was aware of him. She leaned back in her chair, her eyes fixed unseeingly on the television screen, grappling with this unexpected development, and then she forced herself to concentrate on the birds and animals which had been photographed so beautifully.

Gradually the emotion which had surged through her like a leaping flame died down so that when the programme had finished she was able to comment on it intelligently and look straight at Scott without avoiding his gaze. It must have been the heat of the room which had affected her, she told herself, and refused to probe any deeper into her feelings.

"Another drink?" offered Scott, but she shook her head.

"Well, I will. It's been one hell of a day and I'm not sorry it's over."

"Did something go wrong at the factory?" asked Drina.

He grimaced. "There's always something going wrong these days. Labour relations are tricky, and though so far I've managed to sort things out without the threat of a strike it's like walking a tightrope. My grandfather's attitude doesn't help either. Things have changed fundamentally since he was a young man, but he can't realize it and he's impatient with the men's demands for an increase in the basic rate because, to him, they're already drawing enormous wages. I'll be just as rigid, I suppose, when I'm his age, providing I'm still here and the factory's still here, which is problematical."

Drina had never heard him speak like that before, and she willed him to go on. She reminded herself wryly that he was only talking to her because there was no one else at hand and that if Vanessa had been available she would have been the recipient of these confidences, but it didn't seem to matter.

She said impulsively: "Did you choose to go into the factory, or had you ambitions for another career?"

"No, I'm doing what I've always wanted to do. Don't let me give you the impression that my grandfather pushed me into his mould, he didn't. He sent me to the Royal College of Art, then when I'd finished my course there he took me into the factory and started me at the bottom, the best grounding anyone could have. I worked my way up through the various departments until, finally, he put me in charge of design. I'm grateful to him for that, although I can't pretend we always see eye to eye about the end product. To Grandfather, English furniture reached its peak in the eighteenth century, and since then it's declined steadily. I'm willing to worship at the shrine of Chippendale and Hepplewhite, but a well designed modern piece is the antique of the future, and I don't despise industrial design either. You've got to educate people to want furniture which is visually pleasing and at the same time you must be practical and take all kinds of things into account such as form, colour, decoration, texture, fitness for its job, method of production and saleability."

"I've never thought of it like that, but I take your point," agreed Drina, her interest caught. "Even though I knew nothing about furniture then, I admired your chairs the moment I saw them in that boardroom. They looked so right."

"Thank you, that's a great compliment. I shall always have an affection for that particular chair because it won me a Design Centre Award and led to my next commission which was to design bookcases and tables for one of the University libraries. I enjoyed doing that very much."

"And what now? Will you be content to remain at the factory all your life?"

"I'd like to work in a wider sphere for a time at least, but I don't want to see the factory go, and it would grieve my grandfather very much. I shall carry on as I am for the present and let the future take care of itself."

Then with a sharp reversal of mood Scott said: "Good lord, you can't want to listen to me laying down the law about furniture design. I'm apt to get carried away, and forget that everyone isn't as absorbed in it as I am. You shouldn't be such a good listener, Drina."

"But I was enjoying it," protested Drina. "During

these last weeks I've picked up quite a lot from the books your grandfather's been consulting, and it's made me anxious to learn more. By the time his book's finished I should be quite an authority on furniture myself."

"What are you going to do then?" asked Scott abruptly.

"I don't quite know," answered Drina lightly. At the moment she was reluctant to look so far ahead. She had grown to enjoy being at Broomyates, and she didn't want to go back to London. "Something will turn up."

"Probably Don Madderley. Is he coming down for the fancy dress ball?"

"Yes. Lois and Marc are putting him up at the stable flat."

"I see. Excuse me, while I go up to see that my grandfather is all right."

He went out, and Drina sighed. She had been enjoying the conversation, and she wanted to hear a lot more about his ideas and plans for the future. She wondered if he confided them to Vanessa, or if she showed no interest in them. Life couldn't be altogether easy for Scott, living in a house with people of a different generation and trying to fit his life to theirs. He evidently had too much conscience to go away and leave his aunt and grandfather on their own, but would Vanessa be willing to adapt herself to that situation? Drina doubted it, and wondered if the pattern would repeat itself with Scott torn once more between his love for her and his duty to his grandfather.

He came in and announced that his grandfather was asleep, so Drina said: "If you want to go out at all, I'll be here if he needs anything, and your aunt should be back very soon."

Scott glanced at the clock. "So she should. I'd no idea we'd been talking so long."

"Shall I make some coffee? She might be glad of a cup when she comes in."

"That's a good idea. I could do with one myself."

Drina slipped into the kitchen, and switched on the percolator. She found biscuits in a tin, and carried a tray back into the sitting-room.

Scott said lazily : "There's no end to your talents. A good listener, makes marvellous coffee; what more could a man ask?"

"A great deal more, I should think."

"You're too modest. Don Madderley's a fortunate man."

"Why all this harping on Don? We're just good friends."

"I seem to have heard that before, and are you sure that describes his attitude towards you?"

Drina was silent. She had been enjoying this evening so much, but now Scott seemed intent on needling her. Why should he worry about Don's attitude towards her? It couldn't matter to him.

She said slowly: "I like Don, we get on well together. It's nothing more than that."

"No?" queried Scott softly, almost jeeringly, and all at once the air between them was charged with tension. Drina caught her breath and jumped to her feet while in the same instant Scott rose too. They stood facing each other, and Drina could feel her blood pounding as she waited for something, anything, to spark off the explosion between them. Then the front door banged, and Elfrida's voice called : "I'm back at last. Is everything all right?"

"Perfectly," answered Scott calmly, and Drina found

herself trembling as if she were cold. She clenched her teeth to control it, and was able to smile at Elfrida as the older woman came into the room.

"Grandfather was asleep a short while ago," went on Scott. "Drina made some coffee for you, but we seem to have drunk it all."

"I'll make some more," said Drina, glad to escape to the kitchen. She busied herself there with the percolator, wondering what could have come over her. Obviously, Scott hadn't been affected, and the build-up of tension between them had existed only in her own imagination. She was becoming fanciful and ought to take a few days' holiday, only she didn't want to leave Broomyates at present and there wasn't anywhere she really cared to go. She would probably take a break after Easter when the weather would be better.

Don arrived in good time on the Friday of the ball. Drina took him across to the stable flat where Lois had a bowl of creamy celery soup with croutons floating on top of it ready for him.

"I didn't think you'd want a substantial meal now," said Lois. "I've put the electric heater on in your bedroom so that it will be warm for you to change."

"Thank you," he said. "What time do we set out, Drina?"

"Around nine," she answered. "Things won't be swinging until then."

Back in her bedroom, she changed into the blue nylon dress and brushed up her hair, piling it on top of her head and binding it round with a silver ribbon so that a cluster of curls fell from the topknot. Then she made up her face carefully in the way she and Lois had arranged, and slipped her feet into silver sandals. When she was ready she walked across to the stable flat since Don was giving all four of them a lift to the Village Hall. He opened the door to her, looking astonished when he saw her.

"I'd never have believed it," he said. "You and Lois look exactly alike tonight. I know you're twins, but up to now I've easily been able to tell you apart."

"I suppose our bone structure's the same," said Drina, "so when we really want to resemble each other we can manage it under artificial light. It wouldn't be nearly so convincing in daylight."

"We make a good pair of 'Heavenly Twins', don't we?" said Lois. "Take off your wrap, Drina, and stand by me."

"When you stand side by side I can see that Drina's slightly taller and you're rather more blonde," declared Don. "Otherwise there's no difference. What do you say, Marc?"

"They're very alike tonight," agreed Marc, "but I'm sure I'd always be able to tell which was Lois under all circumstances."

"Let's go," said Lois impatiently, and picking up a brilliant Spanish shawl she swathed it round her shoulders before walking out to Don's car.

He drove to the Village Hall and parked round the back, then they made their way to the warmth inside. The hall had been gaily decorated, and banks of flowers and leaves hid the shabbiness of the paintwork. The band was blaring away in fine style, and as soon as the two girls had shed their wraps they made their way to the dance floor. Don claimed Drina, and they moved off together into the crowd.

He was unusually silent, and for the first time she was aware of constraint between them. She wished now that she had never met him on the cruise, or that Scott had never mentioned his Community Centre project so that, once Don had left the ship, there would have been nothing to draw him down to Broomyates. But it was too late for that. She could only hope that no real damage had been done, that both he and Lois would come to their senses.

Unfortunately, at the moment it didn't look much like it. His duty dance over, Don walked across to Lois, and the instant the music started again she was in his arms. Marc said to Drina: "Shall we?" But all the time she was chattering to him she was watching Lois and Don who were circling the floor, gazing raptly at each other. Someone else noticed their absorption—Vanessa, who was dancing with Scott. She didn't comment on it to her partner, however, but determined to keep her eyes on Lois. It might be rewarding.

Drina noticed Scott dancing with Vanessa, and her heart gave a queer little flutter when her eyes met his. In what she imagined was an effort to please Vanessa, he was wearing a white dinner jacket and red cummerbund with his black evening trousers, and he looked very masculine and well-groomed. Vanessa, her head held regally high, was a good foil for him, and having glanced round the rest of the dancers in fancy dress, Drina could see that Vanessa's costume would inevitably take the prize.

She had hoped that Scott might ask her for the next dance but she was claimed by the farmer who sat on the community centre committee, and when he relinquished her Scott had left the room. Drina didn't know that there had been an accident in the kitchen, that one of the voluntary helpers had tripped and banged her head and that Scott had offered to take her home which meant that he was missing from the hall for more than half an hour. As it was, she danced and smiled mechanically without enjoying herself, but it wasn't for some time that she realized that neither Lois nor Don was in the room either. Marc was dancing with Vanessa, and Drina hoped that he hadn't noticed his wife's absence while she wondered uneasily where Lois could be.

Vanessa knew where Scott had gone since she had been with him when he was called to the kitchen, and to fill in the time until he came back, she wasn't adverse to practising her charms on Marc. He didn't see any reason to be rude to her and slap her down, so, although he wasn't attracted to her, he made the bantering rejoinders which were expected of him until she said: "Oh, I've left my cigarettes in the car, and I really can't endure another moment without one. I'm cutting down on smoking, but so far I haven't been able to drop it entirely. How about you?"

"I stopped a while ago," said Marc, forbearing to add that he had had no alternative since he couldn't afford to smoke when he was out of a job, "so I'm afraid I can't offer you one."

"Then we'll go and get mine," said Vanessa. "I'll be glad to have a breath of fresh air. It's terribly stuffy in here."

The atmosphere had certainly warmed up since the dance began, and as it was mild outside Marc was glad of the stroll across to Vanessa's car. She found her cigarettes, lit one, and they stood talking for a few moments before walking back towards the hall. In that brief space of time, Lois and Don had also come out for a breath of fresh air, and as they stood in the angle of the wall of the hall, Don's arms came round Lois and he pulled her into a passionate embrace. She brought her own arms up round his neck, straining her body to his.

For a moment he raised his head, whispering thickly: "Oh, Lois, Lois!" and then his mouth was on hers again and they were lost to everything but each other.

It was at this moment that Vanessa and Marc walked past the side of the hall. Vanessa, being on the inside, saw them first and realized at once that it was Lois, but Marc was almost past them when in the dim light he saw the blur of blue nylon with the gleam of golden hair above it. He gave a smothered exclamation, but Vanessa grabbed his arm and hurried him on.

"Don't stop," she hissed. "You'll only embarrass them. Drina must be fathoms deep in love to stand kissing in such a conspicuous spot."

"Drina," repeated Marc in bewilderment, "but I thought it was Lois," and then full realization dawned and he wrenched his arm out of Vanessa's grasp and turned back.

But he wasn't quite quick enough. Don had caught sight of Vanessa and Marc, and he had pulled Lois rapidly in the opposite direction through a fire escape door which had been left open for air.

"Was it Marc?" she gasped, and he answered: "Yes, with Vanessa. Don't worry, I'm almost sure he didn't see you, and if he did, it isn't a hanging matter."

"You don't know Marc. You mightn't think it, but he's dreadfully jealous." Abruptly transported from bliss to fear, she was in a state of panic. "Don, what am I to do? Marc will never believe that we were only having a bit of fun."

"I've told you, I'm almost sure he didn't see you." But Don couldn't keep a note of doubt out of his voice. "Come back to the dance floor."

"No, not that. You go into the hall, and I'll slip into the ladies' cloakroom."

Once there, Lois repaired her make-up with a trembling hand, then stood undecided what to do next. She couldn't stay in the cloakroom for the rest of the evening, but she dreaded returning to the hall to face an accusing Marc. As she hesitated Vanessa came in, and one look at her face told Lois that there was trouble ahead.

"There you are, Lois," she said. "I wanted a word with you," and Lois followed her into the passage.

"Is it Marc?" Lois faltered, and Vanessa nodded.

"He saw you and Don in each other's arms outside. What possessed you to stand there kissing madly where everyone could see you?"

"We acted on impulse," Lois defended herself, "and I never expected Marc to come past at that identical moment. It didn't mean anything but a passing pleasure, either to Don or to me."

"I don't think Marc is going to accept that easily," said Vanessa dryly. "I assured him that it was Drina kissing Don and not you, but I didn't really convince him. You'll have to do that."

"But how can I if he's already suspicious? There was an episode in Ibiza, quite harmless, but Marc was furious with me for days."

"You'll have to enlist Drina's help, of course," said Vanessa thoughtfully. "After all, Don's supposed to be her friend, isn't he, so what more natural than that the two of them should be locked in a passionate embrace? What would make your statement really watertight would be the announcement of their engagement. That would set all Marc's doubts at rest."

"But I can't see any possibility of their becoming engaged," said Lois miserably. "They're just good friends."

"Well, surely for your sake they'd pretend otherwise for the present. An engagement isn't binding. It can be broken off at any time."

"Drina would hate the deception. It isn't fair to ask her."

Vanessa shrugged. "It's up to you. Now we'd better go back into the hall or Marc will be sending out a search party for you."

Lois walked miserably back to the hall, and glanced round. She noted with relief that Don and Drina were dancing together, and then her heart gave a frightened leap as she saw Marc stalking towards her. His face was set in a white mask, and she could tell that he was furiously angry. He caught hold of her arm, and said savagely : "I want an explanation from you, Lois."

"I don't know what you mean," she faltered. "Please let go my arm, people are staring at us."

"Don't pretend you don't understand me," but he loosened his grip. "Come along, we're going home."

"We can't do that. We came with Drina and Don, and we'll spoil things for them if we say we want to go home now. Let's dance."

"Dance? After what I saw?"

Marc's mouth set in a hard line as he turned abruptly and left her. Lois stared after him with frightened eyes. He would never forgive her for this; it would be impossible to convince him that though she had been attracted by Don, she wasn't in love with him. Don had shown that he in turn was attracted by her, and she hadn't been able to resist the heady thrill of a mild affair. She had never intended to put her marriage into jeopardy, and she was appalled at the prospect which lay ahead.

As the dance ended she sped in a panic across the room to where Drina and Don were standing together.

"You must help me," she babbled. "Don, Marc saw us outside, and he's furious. Vanessa told him that it was Drina he saw and not me, but he won't believe that, not unless he has proof. Drina, you must pretend that you and Don are engaged. It's the only solution, and it could soon be broken off."

Drina stared at her in bewilderment. "What are you talking about? You know there's no question of an engagement between Don and me."

"Look," said Don quickly. "It's a bit awkward. The fact is that Lois and I were outside together a little while ago when Marc and Vanessa walked past. It was all quite harmless, but it would be a bit difficult to convince Marc of that."

"Outside?" repeated Drina, and then comprehension dawned. "Oh, I see."

"Vanessa suggested that if you told Marc that you and Don were engaged he'd believe then that it was you he saw and not me. You will do that for me, won't you, Drina? I know I've been foolish, but I never meant to cause any trouble, and it wouldn't make any difference to you to pretend to be engaged just for a little while."

"I'm willing, Drina, if you are," said Don. "As Lois said, we need only keep up the fiction for a short time, and it would solve things for her."

Drina looked at him steadily. "And for you too. You're as much to blame as she is. Neither of you bothered to consider anyone but yourselves when you decided to have your little bit of fun, so I don't see why I should involve myself and come to the rescue now. Tell Marc the truth, Lois. He loves you, and he'll believe you."

"I can't, I can't. Please help me, Drina. I daren't face him if you don't, and he's coming across to us now."

Lois's eyes widened imploringly, and as Marc reached them, she directed one last glance of frantic appeal at her sister. Then she turned to him and tried to smile.

He said curtly: "They're going to have the fancy dress parade now and then I propose that we push off. I've had enough."

He didn't look at Lois, but she took a deep breath and said: "Drina's got some news for us. She and Don are engaged."

Marc's face registered the shock he felt. "Drina and Don?"

"Yes," answered Don. "Aren't you going to congratulate me?"

"Yes, of course." Marc's voice was quite different now. There was incredulity in it, and apology as he looked at Lois. "I thought ... but that doesn't matter now."

Drina said nothing at all. She should have spoken at once, but she couldn't brand Lois as a liar in front of her husband.

She said after a moment: "Do we need to wait for the fancy dress parade? Vanessa's bound to win it, and I think I've had enough too. I'll go for my wrap."

She didn't wait for Lois, wanting to be alone for a moment, and as she turned into the corridor she bumped into Scott.

He said ruefully: "I've been hoping for a dance with you, but there was an accident in the kitchen and I had to take the victim home. Is it time for the parade?"

"Yes," replied Drina, "but I'm not waiting for it."

"You're leaving now?"

Marc behind her answered for her. "We're going back to the flat to have a celebratory drink. Drina and Don have just become engaged."

"Engaged?" repeated Scott, and now he was looking at her in quite a different way. "I hope you'll be very happy."

"Thank you," said Drina tonelessly, and in that instant she discovered that she loved Scott, deeply and for ever, Scott who believed she was engaged to Don and who was going to marry Vanessa.

CHAPTER EIGHT

THEY went back to the stable flat, and Marc, who was exuberant in his relief that it was Drina who was involved with Don and not Lois, insisted on pouring drinks for all of them. Drina wanted nothing so much as to go back to Broomyates, but she realized that this might arouse Marc's suspicions, so she played her part and managed to smile up at Don when he put his arm around her shoulders.

At last, however, she was able to break away, and Don walked across the garden to the house with her. As soon as they were out of earshot of the flat he said sheepishly : "Drina, I'm sorry for what's happened. I never meant to complicate matters like this, but Lois is so attractive and responsive that—well, I lost my head."

"I acknowledge that she went half way to meet you, but you're older and more experienced than she is, Don. It was madness for the pair of you to behave like that right outside the hall."

"I realize that now, but no real harm's been done."

"Except that we're all deceiving Marc, and I don't like telling lies to him or to the other people who think that we're engaged. It puts me in a very awkward position."

"I can see that," he admitted, "but in a few weeks we can break it off by mutual consent. Or we can let it stand if you like. I'm very fond of you, Drina. You're just as attractive as Lois in a different way."

"You don't expect me to be flattered by a proposal

like that, I hope," said Drina crisply. "I've no intention of marrying you, Don, because I'm not in love with you and I never shall be."

"You needn't sound as if I'd insulted you," said Don aggrievedly.

"You can't call it anything else when you're caught kissing a girl one moment and then, a couple of hours later, you're quite willing to transfer your affections to her sister."

"All right, I get the point," said Don sulkily. "I take it that you'd prefer me to make an excuse to go back to London tomorrow morning after breakfast?"

"Yes, I would. Good night."

Drina let herself into the house, and went silently up to her room. She went to bed and lay there, staring into the darkness, until after a considerable interval she heard the front door close and Scott's footsteps on the landing. The ball must have ended some time ago, but it wasn't difficult to guess where he had been. He would have taken Vanessa home and stayed on at her house. Drina tried not to picture them in each other's arms, but it was dawn before she dozed off at last. Because of this she overslept, and was late going down to breakfast. The others had finished, but Elfrida came in with a rack of fresh toast.

"I'm sorry I'm late," apologized Drina. "I'm afraid it was a long time before I got to sleep last night."

"That's hardly surprising," said Elfrida archly. "You must have been too excited. Scott told us your news."

"My news?" echoed Drina stupidly.

"About your engagement. Of course I wasn't exactly unprepared for it, but it gave Father a jolt. Naturally, he doesn't want to lose your services, but I told him not to be selfish. He's in the study now, so would you go in as soon as you've finished your breakfast?"

Drina drank a cup of coffee, crumbled a piece of toast, and then braced herself to open the study door. Mr. Carlyon glared at her as she entered.

"Scott tells me that you and young Madderley announced your engagment at the dance last night. I'm disappointed in you, Drina. He isn't the man for you."

"We're not proposing to get married yet," said Drina evasively.

"And never will, if you've any sense. Why did you have to be so precipitate? You know my plans."

"But you can't expect everyone to fall in with them, Mr. Carlyon."

He ignored this. "I suppose you'll want the weekend off to go gallivanting with your fiancé. I wanted you to work this morning so that we could finish that chapter on Chippendale."

"Don has to return to London so that I'm quite willing to work if I may have ten minutes now to say goodbye to him."

"Very well, get along with you. I'll expect you back here in a quarter of an hour."

Drina ran across to the stable flat where Don was finishing his breakfast. With his easy-going temperament it was impossible for him to remain depressed for long, and he had recovered his spirits completely this morning.

"Hallo, darling," he said, standing up. He put his arms round Drina and gave her a hearty kiss to which she submitted since Marc was standing by the window.

Marc grinned, and said : "I'll leave you two to your

fond farewells. It's a pity Don has to return to London, Drina, otherwise you could have gone out together for the day. It's going to be sunny."

"As it happens, Mr. Carlyon wants me to work this morning," answered Drina. "He's anxious to finish the current chapter of the book."

Marc went out, and Drina said: "Goodbye, Don."

"Only for the present," he countered. "I'll be in touch. After all, we are supposed to be engaged, so we must make it convincing for a while at least. I'll give you a ring tonight."

She had to admit that it would look peculiar if he didn't, so she said: "Very well, about six. Are you ready to leave now?"

"Yes, so you'd better walk out to the car with me."

Drina saw him off, and then went back to the study.

"At last," grumbled Mr. Carlyon. "Come along, there's plenty to do."

He kept her hard at it for the rest of the morning as a sign that he was annoyed since it wasn't often they worked on a Saturday, and there was no real urgency to finish the chapter. By the next day Mr. Carlyon had more or less recovered his temper, but Scott was cool and withdrawn and Drina was wretchedly aware that their growing friendship had been abruptly terminated. It was as if these last weeks when he had mellowed towards her had been wiped out, and she found this doubly hard to endure because her feelings towards him had changed completely.

At the beginning, she had disliked Scott as much as he had disliked her; now she was in love with him and couldn't bear his chilly indifference. Why the news of her engagement should have changed his attitude towards her she was at a loss to understand, unless his reaction was due to disgust. She remembered, now, that he had never seemed enthusiastic about Don, and that night they had dined together she had told him that there was no more than friendship between Don and herself. Now they were engaged, and Scott must think that she would say anything which suited her purpose, perhaps he even suspected that she'd been encouraging him to flirt with her.

She writhed inwardly at the injustice of this, but her conclusion was confirmed when, a few days later, Vanessa dropped in to ask Scott to check the caterer's expense accounts for the ball. There was no need for this since Drina had already checked them, but Vanessa obviously welcomed an excuse to call at Broomyates.

Scott offered her a drink, and she settled herself in a corner of the sofa, her long, lovely legs displayed to maximum advantage. Mr. Carlyon had been taken to play bridge with an old friend, and Elfrida was visiting Joan Priddy, so for once Drina welcomed the advent of the other girl since she hadn't wanted a *tête-à-tête* evening with Scott under present circumstances.

"I suppose you'll be going back to London now, Drina?" remarked Vanessa casually. "With Don based there, it wouldn't be much fun for you here. You'd see hardly anything of each other."

Since Vanessa was aware of the real situation, this was a body blow which Drina hadn't anticipated. With a sense of shock she realized that the other girl wanted her to leave Broomyates, but before she could work out the implication of this, Scott said : "One can never be sure what Drina will do. She weighs things up very carefully before she acts."

This was even more unexpected than the other, and Drina felt physically sick. Vanessa said sweetly : "Oh, Scott, that's rather severe. It makes Drina sound so calculating," but a tiny smile of triumph curved her mouth.

She began to chatter about summer holidays, discussing various places with Scott and almost ignoring Drina now that she had made her point. Before long, Drina made an excuse to leave the room and went up to her bedroom. Scott had shown his opinion of her so plainly that this must be the end. She couldn't endure to stay in the same house with him under these conditions, which meant she must go, and she resolved to ask Mr. Carlyon to release her from her contract the very next day.

She waited until she was driving him to the factory the following morning, and then she said baldly: "Mr. Carlyon, I'd like to leave Broomyates and go back to London. I know I promised to stay until the first draft of the book was completed, but I'm asking you to waive that condition."

He turned his head sharply, gave her a searching look, and then said flatly: "No, I intend to keep you to our agreement. The book's progressing well, and I don't want any hold-ups at this stage. You must stay until the first draft's finished. The fact that you've decided to get engaged to that fellow doesn't entitle you to rearrange matters to suit yourself."

"No, of course not, but I'd be very grateful if you'd allow me to go," pleaded Drina desperately. "If I'm here and Don is in London, we shan't be able to see very much of each other."

She hated pretending that this was her reason for wanting to leave Broomyates, but she couldn't tell Mr. Carlyon the truth. As she tried to think of an argument which would move him, he added: "If you've time to think things over perhaps you'll come to your senses. Madderley isn't the man for you, and I don't want

Scott to marry Vanessa. You and Scott are made for each other, if only you weren't both so stupid that you can't see it."

Drina was seized with a strong desire to laugh and cry, both at the same time. Mr. Carlyon was right as far as she was concerned, but she couldn't tell him so. She made one last bid for her freedom.

"If you'd agree to my going in a month's time," she began, but he interrupted her.

"Don't argue with me any more, it's quite useless. You must stay until the first draft of the book's in order, and you can hand over to someone else. That's my final word."

She gave in, because there was nothing else she could do. If she'd been of a different nature, she would simply have packed her case and left because Mr. Carlyon couldn't restrain her physically, but she had too much sense of honour to do that. She had given her word to stay a certain length of time, and unless Mr. Carlyon released her from her promise she couldn't go back on it. Somehow she would have to endure Scott's chilly scorn until his grandfather agreed to let her go.

She tried not to let her unhappiness show, but she and Lois were always sensitive to each other's moods and her sister said: "Are you still worrying about your phoney engagement?"

"Yes," admitted Drina. "I loathe playing a part, and I'm very bad at it. Now all this has happened I'd prefer to leave Broomyates and go back to London."

"Well, you've got a good excuse. Tell Mr. Carlyon that you don't want to be so far away from Don."

"I've tried that, but it didn't work," said Drina wryly. "When I took this job I promised to stay until the first draft of the book was finished, and Mr.

Carlyon's holding me to that. He's quite entitled to do it, but I hoped he wouldn't.''

"Oh,'' Lois was disconcerted. "He oughtn't to want to keep you against your will. I wish he would let you go, and then perhaps I could persuade Marc to go back to London too.''

"But he's doing so well down here,'' said Drina quickly, "and enjoying the work. He probably wouldn't find nearly such a congenial job in London.''

Lois said complainingly : "But there's nobody interesting to meet here, and nowhere to go. It's so different in London.''

"You weren't thinking of getting in touch with Don again?'' asked Drina searchingly.

"Oh, no,'' said Lois hurriedly. "That's all over, but I prefer to live in a place where there's some life.''

"Well, you'll have to stick it out in Lindisthorpe a while longer, and so shall I.''

At the boutique the next day Vanessa remarked casually that she didn't suppose Drina would be staying on at Broomyates now, and Lois unsuspectingly poured out the tale of Mr. Carlyon's tyranny.

"That's too bad,'' said Vanessa commiseratingly. "Men of Mr. Carlyon's age who have been used to a good deal of their own way often never consider other people's feelings. I must see if I can't do something for your sister. I'm sure Scott would put in a word for her.''

She'd hoped that Drina would want to return to London, and was annoyed that Robert Carlyon should prove obstructive. It would be useless for her to appeal to him when he disliked her so much that she was sure he would keep Drina at Broomyates if only to spite her, Vanessa, but it shouldn't be difficult to enlist Scott's help after the remark he had made about Drina that evening. Vanessa had speculated from time to time whether Scott was really blind to Drina's attractions, and even recalling his unfavourable comment on her it didn't pay to take any risks. The sooner Drina left Broomyates the better Vanessa would like it.

She rang Scott that afternoon to ask him to drop in.

"I can't talk freely over the telephone," she said, "so could you spare me a few minutes this evening? Come after dinner and we'll have a cosy drink by the fire."

"Very well," he agreed. "I'll be there about eight."

There was a leaping log fire and a tempting tray of drinks to greet him. Vanessa was looking seductive in a leopard-printed velvet lounging suit, and she sat down on the sofa, patting the cushion beside her.

"Pour me a vodka and tonic and then we can talk," she said.

"What is this important matter you have to discuss with me?" enquired Scott. "You sounded very mysterious over the telephone."

"I couldn't explain with Lois within earshot because it concerns her sister. Did you know that Drina had told your grandfather that she wanted to leave Broomyates and go back to London?"

Scott poured himself a whisky and soda. "No, I didn't know that."

"Apparently, your grandfather refused to let her go. It appears that when she took the job she promised to stay on until the first draft of the book was finished, and he's holding her to that. It's rather unreasonable, don't you think?"

"Grandfather isn't a particularly reasonable man."

"That's an understatement, as we both know. The point is, Scott, couldn't you use your influence to persuade him to let Drina go? She's just become engaged, and you really can't expect her fiancé to trail down here every time he wants to see her."

"It isn't the end of the earth," pointed out Scott.

Vanessa frowned. "You mean you won't help?"

"I mean that I've no intention of interfering with my grandfather's affairs. He employs Drina, not me."

"I see." With a great effort Vanessa controlled her temper, and even managed to smile. "I'm afraid I've dragged you out here for nothing. Would you like to listen to some new records I've bought, or talk?"

In the end, they did both and Vanessa was able to congratulate herself that at least Scott stayed on, but at the same time she felt uneasy about his rejection of her suggestion that he should persuade his grandfather to let Drina go. Was it really because he thought the old man should be allowed to run his own affairs, or did he, in fact, want Drina to stay on at Broomyates? It was ridiculous to suppose that he had any feeling at all for her, but Vanessa was aware that there were depths in Scott to which she had never penetrated and she couldn't rule out the possibility that Drina was the type to appeal to him.

Part of his attraction for Vanessa lay in the fact that when they'd met again he hadn't immediately succumbed to her charm. The adoring youth she remembered had been replaced by a mature man whose calm appraisal of her had intrigued her, accustomed as she was to all the men of her acquaintance vying for her favours, and she was determined to have his heart at her feet also. Because of that she intended to eliminate all possible rivals, and Drina headed the list. If she couldn't be got rid of in a straightforward manner, then guile would have to be employed. Vanessa began to think hard.

But Scott wasn't the only complication in Drina's life. She was finding it increasingly difficult to fob off Don who seemed more and more prepared to regard this shock engagement as the real thing. He was spending most of his weekends in the Lake District, supervising the conversion of two stone cottages into a desirable residence for a wealthy manufacturer, and he had formed the habit of ringing Drina two or three times a week. Because she couldn't protest much on the telephone where she was likely to be overheard, she wrote and told him that he must curtail his calls instead of increasing them, but he ignored her letters, and began to treat her as if they really were engaged and would be married eventually.

Finally she walked down to a telephone box in the village, and, managing to get through to him, prepared for a battle.

"Don," she said, "you're behaving ridiculously. Naturally I expected you to ring at first to keep up the fiction that we were engaged, but the idea was that before long it should be broken off. I'm not engaged to you and I never shall be, so please don't make it all the more difficult."

"I've been thinking things over," he answered, "and I can see what a fool I've been. It was you all the time, Drina, but you never gave me much encouragement and Lois did. I don't mean that I blame her for what happened. It was quite as much my fault, but it was only a game for both of us. My feeling for you is different, and I shall continue to ring you up."

As Easter approached, Scott remained aloof, and Drina's unhappiness was a fierce ache which didn't subside as the days went by. She was concentrating on finishing the book as quickly as possible, but although it was making steady progress there was still a lot to be done before the first draft was completed. To distract her mind from her troubles, she was taking a keen interest in Elfrida's preparations for the Flower

Festival. Elfrida and Joan Priddy had drawn up their plan of campaign, and arranged that one of the leading florists in the market at Canterbridge should obtain a special consignment of flowers which would be flown in from Jersey for them.

"It will mean us going in to Canterbridge to collect them at six o'clock on the morning of Easter Saturday," said Elfrida. "Perhaps we could get someone to open up the church so that we could take the flowers straight there."

"Why not let me drive you into Canterbridge," suggested Drina, "while Miss Priddy goes to the church? She knows exactly what you'll need, so she could assemble everything in readiness."

"That's a good idea if you don't mind getting up so early. I've planned a special arrangement in the north window, and I'm ordering four dozen roses for that alone."

"It should look most effective."

Elfrida was a different person these days, absorbed in the preparations for the Flower Festival, and with more confidence than ever before. She had certainly blossomed during these last weeks, and had lost her deprecating manner.

Don telephoned to ask Drina to go up to London for the Easter weekend, and was put out when she told him that it was impossible since she would be helping with the Flower Festival.

"Surely you don't have to work all day Saturday and Sunday," he protested.

"I don't *have* to do anything," she told him, "but I want to help. I'm very anxious for Miss Carlyon's sake that the Festival should be a success."

"But I thought we could have fun together, whoop it up a bit. You've never given me a chance to show that I regret what happened at the fancy dress ball."

"It isn't necessary; I believe you," said Drina quickly.

"But I want to talk to you properly, make you understand that we could pick up our relationship where we left it after the cruise."

"That would be impossible. There's no future in it for either of us."

"I've changed," Don persisted obstinately, "and if we met you'd realize it. Since you won't come to me, then I must come to you. I'll stay in Canterbridge over the weekend and take you out to dinner."

"No, Don, I don't want to go out with you."

"I'm coming down," he repeated.

"Then I shall refuse to see you."

Drina meant what she said, and Don evidently realized it because he paused, then said: "Look, let's compromise. I'll come down on Good Friday, take you out to dinner in the evening so that we can talk properly, and then if you really don't want to see me again I'll accept your decision, go back to London, and you can break off the engagement. That's fair, isn't it?"

"I suppose it is," agreed Drina reluctantly. "Very well then, I'll see you on Good Friday in the evening."

"I'll book a room in Canterbridge for Friday night, and pick you up about eight."

Don rang off, and Drina went across to the stable flat to tell Lois of his forthcoming visit.

"This will be the final one," she said, "and then the whole episode can be forgotten. I don't want to go out with Don, but if I do I can at least pretend that we had a row and broke off the engagement."

"You might change your mind about that," said Lois.

Drina shook her head. "Oh, no."

"There's a lot to be said for Don. He's attractive, good company, even-tempered and generous."

"But I'm not in love with him and I never shall be."

"It seems a pity," said Lois pensively.

At the boutique the next morning, when trade was slack, she snatched ten minutes to brew two cups of instant coffee in the little room at the back, and sipping hers, Vanessa asked casually: "Is your sister taking a holiday at Easter?"

"No, she's helping with the Flower Festival at the church, and going early to the market on Saturday morning to collect the flowers."

"I'm afraid I haven't had anything to do with the Flower Festival. It's Elfrida's project, and she's kept it very much to herself."

"Don wanted Drina to go up to London for the weekend, but when she explained that she couldn't get away he arranged to come down here instead. He's taking Drina to dine at the Country Club on Friday night."

"How very nice." Vanessa put down her coffee cup. "Perhaps you didn't do your sister such a bad turn, after all, when you asked her to pretend that she was engaged to Don. It may prove to be true in the end."

"I don't think so," said Lois regretfully. "Drina's quite insistent that she isn't in love with Don and never will be. It makes me wonder if she hasn't fallen for someone else."

"It could be," agreed Vanessa, and then a customer came into the boutique and Lois moved forward to attend her.

Left alone for a moment, Vanessa's face set into hard lines. It looked very much to her also as if Drina had fallen for another man, and if that were the case it could be Scott. That meant she must make every effort to get Drina away from Broomyates in the very near future.

She frowned as she began to ponder a plan of campaign. Life must be made utterly untenable for Drina at Broomyates, and at the same time, something must happen to turn Scott even further against her. Vanessa went over in her mind what Lois had just told her, and a glimmer of an idea came to her. She would need the co-operation of the man who came to do her garden, but it shouldn't be difficult to achieve that. He would undertake anything for a cash bonus, so she would have a word with him the next day.

Suddenly Easter was upon them, and Elfrida was geared into feverish activity, desperately anxious that nothing should go wrong. She spent the Thursday down at the church making sure that everything was in readiness for the decorating on Saturday, and came home tired out.

"You're doing too much," said Drina. "You'll be a wreck before the Festival starts."

"It's stupid of me, I know," admitted Elfrida, "but I'm so afraid I've forgotten something vital. It's the first time I've ever undertaken anything like this, and I do want it to be a success."

"I'm sure it will be," said Drina.

"I'm spending tomorrow evening with Joan and staying the night there as we thought that would be easier since we have to be up so early the next morning. You're sure you'll manage to wake in time?"

"I'll be at Miss Priddy's house on the dot of six," promised Drina. "I'm going out to the Country Club tomorrow with Don, but we shan't make it a late evening. He's staying the night in Canterbridge."

"Not at the stable flat?"

"No, he didn't want to impose on Lois."

Elfrida looked surprised but didn't say anything more. Drina reflected wryly that she would be even more astonished when she heard that the engagement was broken off, but it couldn't be helped.

The next evening she wore her scarlet dress, and after Don had tucked her carefully into the car they drove out to the Country Club. It was a miserable night, cold and bleak with driving rain which showed no sign of easing off, and Drina had to dash for the shelter of the hotel under an umbrella held over her by Don. As she hurried inside, she saw a man lurking at the entrance to the car park, and she had a vague feeling that she had seen him before, but couldn't remember where. He wore a shabby anorak with the hood pulled up over his head, and, as she stepped inside the hotel, she saw him sidle into the car park and begin to thread his way through the cars.

Inside, there was warmth and light, and she forgot all about the man as they were shown to the table Don had booked. He ordered lavishly, and when she protested at his extravagance he said : "It's to show you that I'd like to spend my life giving you everything you want."

"Now you're being silly," she said severely. "I agreed to come out with you tonight because it seemed only fair, but this really is the end, Don."

"But why be so final? All right, break off the engagment if you must, but when you return to London in a few months' time surely we can get together again?"

"You'll have forgotten me by then."

"Never," he protested.

"It didn't take you long to substitute Lois for me," pointed out Drina.

"That was only a bit of fun," he demurred. "It wasn't serious."

"And neither is your feeling for me. In six months you'll hardly remember me."

"You haven't a very high opinion of me," said Don aggrievedly. "I suppose I could scarcely hope to measure up to Scott Carlyon, though heaven knows what he's got to be so high and mighty about."

"You're jealous of him, aren't you?" said Drina slowly.

"Not jealous, but infuriated at the way women seem to fall for him. I know only too well why you cooled off me, Drina. It was because you're besotted with him. Well, you won't get him. Vanessa will see to that."

This was said with a malice which repelled Drina, and made her thankful that she wouldn't be seeing Don again. She said spiritedly: "You were eager enough to come down here in the hope of getting the contract for the community centre for your firm. You weren't critical of Scott then."

"Our tender's been rejected, so I'm free to say what I like about him now," returned Don unpleasantly, and Drina rose to her feet.

"Not in front of me, because I won't sit here and listen to you. I'd like to go home, please."

"Not yet, we're only half way through the meal," he protested.

"Then change the subject."

"Oh, very well," he submitted sulkily.

The rest of the meal was punctuated with bursts of conversation followed by uncomfortable pauses. Drina didn't enjoy it in the least, and as soon as they'd drunk their coffee she rose to her feet again.

"I'd like to go now, Don. I don't think either of us is enjoying this."

"I'm certainly not," he conceded. "God, doesn't it do anything but rain in this place?"

Outside, it was wetter than ever, with the wind rising to add to the miseries of the night. Don tried to hold the umbrella over Drina as they dashed for the car park, but both of them were quite damp by the time they reached the car and she was glad to pull the rug round her as they started off.

"I take it that you're staying at the White Swan," she remarked as they drove out into the main road.

"I'm not staying anywhere," returned Don shortly, peering through the streaming windscreen. "I've decided to go back to London tonight."

"But I thought you'd booked a room in Canterbridge? It's not fit to drive far in this weather."

"I prefer it to staying any longer in this hole. As soon as I've dropped you I'm going back to my flat and civilization."

Drina said no more, and the car turned into a winding country lane without lights and with trees arching overhead. The wind howling through their branches made an eerie sound, and she shivered. The sooner she was back at Broomyates the better she would like it. It had been a disastrous evening, and she'd have done far better to stick to her original resolve not to go out again with Don. The only good thing was that he no longer wanted to marry her, and she could announce the breaking of her mock engagement with a clear conscience.

Half way along the lane, the car spluttered and stopped. Don cursed, then looked incredulously at the petrol gauge.

"We can't be out of petrol," he said. "I filled her up on the journey here today."

For a moment Drina thought of the old trick of pretending to run out of petrol, then she could see that Don was genuinely astonished. Besides, he wouldn't have tried that trick tonight. He'd no more desire to linger over the journey to Broomyates than she had. He was no eager lover anxious for a quick embrace; he wanted to get back to London.

"Perhaps your tank's leaking?" suggested Drina.

"I suppose it must be that. I'd better take a look."

Reluctantly he got out of the car, but was back again almost immediately.

"There's no sign or smell of petrol on the road."

"Then you must have forgotten to fill up."

"Damn it, I'm not mental. I know whether I did a thing or not. I filled up with petrol this afternoon, and the car's never been out of my sight since then, except when we were having dinner. All I can think of is that some joker crept into the car park at the Country Club and siphoned the petrol out."

"But why choose your car? It wasn't the end one, or particularly conspicuous."

"Heaven knows why. The fact remains that we're stuck here, miles from anywhere."

"But what are we going to do?" asked Drina anxiously. "We can't stay here all night."

Don shrugged. "It looks as if we shall have to."

"But we can't. They'll be wondering at Broomyates what's happened to me, and. . . ." The full horror of her situation broke over her. "I'm due to go to the market in Canterbridge at six o'clock tomorrow morning to collect the flowers for Elfrida. I can't let her down."

"I don't see that you've any alternative. It's pouring with rain and blowing a gale outside, and I've no intention of contracting pneumonia by struggling to the nearest garage, even if I knew where it was, which I don't."

"But you could find a telephone and ring

Broomyates," Drina pleaded. "Scott would come out for us."

"Let him worry, it'll do him good," said Don callously. "It might knock some of that superiority out of him."

"You're vile!" flashed Drina. "If you won't go, then I will."

"Suit yourself." Don leaned back in his seat. "You won't have gone a hundred yards before you're soaked to the skin, and if you did manage to knock someone up at a house it would be difficult to explain your appearance, wouldn't it?"

Drina opened the door of the car, then drew back from the lashing rain. She was wearing a brocade jacket over her scarlet dress and silver sandals which would be reduced to pulp after five minutes of this weather. Don was right.

It was the most miserable night she had ever spent. Cold and cramped, she huddled in her seat and longed for the dawn. She didn't know whether Don slept or not, but he made no attempt to speak to her, for which she was thankful. It was in the early hours of the morning that she remembered the man in the car park, and it flashed across her mind that he was extraordinarily like Vanessa's gardener. It was absurd, of course, to think it could have been him. She must have been mistaken.

At six o'clock, a lorry loaded with milk came past, and the driver promised to telephone a garage from the nearest box. After what seemed hours, a breakdown van arrived, and the mechanic filled up Don's car from a can. It was eight o'clock when they reached Broomyates, and Drina said: "Before you go on your way I could make you a cup of coffee at the stable flat."

"Don't bother," answered Don. "I'll get some break-fast on the way. Goodbye, Drina." And, as soon as she was out of the car, he roared off.

She fitted her key into the lock, but before she could turn it the door swung open and Scott stood there. She'd seen him angry before, but never in such an icy rage. His eyes raked her contemptuously, taking in her smudged make-up and crumpled dress, then he said: "I wondered you bothered to come back at all, or did Madderley decide that one night was quite sufficient?"

CHAPTER NINE

FOR a moment Drina was rendered speechless by the sheer savagery of his manner. She had expected him to be annoyed by the fact that she had let Elfrida down, but she hadn't anticipated that he would accuse her of having deliberately stayed out all night.

She said: "We ran out of petrol when we were on the way back from the Country Club. Not a soul passed us, and it was such a dreadful night that neither of us could leave the car and walk to a garage to fetch a can of petrol. I've been so worried about letting your aunt down when I'd promised to get up early and drive to the market for the flowers. I could go there now as soon as I've changed my clothes and had a cup of coffee."

"The flowers are at the church. When you didn't return home last night I was determined that Elfrida shouldn't suffer, so I took your place."

He walked away, leaving Drina standing there numbed with shock. In a few moments she pulled herself together and climbed the stairs wearily to her room where she pulled off her clothes and, wrapping herself in her dressing gown, went to run a bath. Lying back in the steaming water, she realized that this was the end. The atmosphere between Scott and herself had been strained ever since the announcement of her engagement to Don; now it would be intolerable. She couldn't go on living at Broomyates under those conditions. She loved Scott, she was afraid she would always love him, but since he didn't trust her, the best thing was for her to go away.

The bath revived her a little, and she dressed as quickly as possible, then went down to the dining-room. The thought of food revolted her, but the coffee percolator was standing on the sideboard and she poured herself a cup. She drank it, then put on her coat and walked down to the church.

Elfrida and Joan Priddy were there with several other helpers, and as soon as she caught sight of Drina, Elfrida said: "Are you all right, Drina? When Scott called for me this morning he said you'd been delayed, and I wondered if anything had gone wrong last night."

"It did," answered Drina. "Don and I left the Country Club about ten, but when we'd travelled five miles and were driving along one of the side lanes, the car ran out of petrol. It was a dreadful night, pouring with rain and blowing a gale, so neither of us could walk to the nearest garage for help, and we had to sit there until a milk lorry from the farm came along around six. The driver left a message with the first garage he came to, and eventually someone came out to our rescue."

"Oh, how wretched for you," sympathized Elfrida. "I'm glad I didn't know you were missing, or I should have been worrying in case you'd had an accident. Scott must have been distracted; I can see now why he looked so grim when he came for me this morning. Are you all right? Shouldn't you be in bed instead of down here?"

"No, I'm not sleepy, and I want to help. What shall I do first?"

"Could you sort the flowers according to the plan at the back of the church?"

Drina worked in the church all day, and by evening it had been transformed into a mass of colour and beauty. Everywhere banks of flowers glowed against the stone walls, and tiny, delicate posies adorned the lectern and pulpit and were strewn along the pews.

"I never dreamed it could look like this," said Drina as Elfrida stood proudly surveying the finished effect.

"I can't take the entire credit," she said deprecatingly. "The colour schemes for the festivals of the church year I took from a book which was recommended to Joan by a friend, but one or two ideas are my own. I particularly like the north window, don't you?"

It represented Advent, and was filled with a great wheel of roses in every shade of scarlet, crimson and vermilion which had an impact on the eye akin to a fanfare of trumpets on the ear.

"It's wonderful," agreed Drina, then fatigue took possession of her, and she closed her eyes.

"You're tired out," said Elfrida, "and so am I. Let's go home."

Scott wasn't in to dinner, and Drina wondered if he were out with Vanessa, but she was too weary to care. She went to bed early and slept, waking to a dull heaviness which made her disinclined to face the day. She spent most of it in the church, taking money from the visitors who came to see the flowers, and the pattern was repeated on the Monday. That evening they counted the takings, and Elfrida reported jubilantly that the profits were far higher than anyone had anticipated.

"A very high proportion of people came in from Canterbridge," she said, "and the Vicar of St. Mary's asked me if I'd decorate his church in August when it celebrates its tercentenary."

"Did you agree to do it?"

"Well, yes, I did. I've also been asked to give some evening lectures on flower arranging, but I don't know whether I could manage it. I haven't had any experience in lecturing."

"But you've got a natural gift with flowers. The success of the Festival this weekend proves it."

"I suppose it does. I think I'll accept the challenge of the lectures," and Elfrida fairly glowed with happiness.

But if she were triumphant at last, Drina wasn't. Once the Festival was over and she had time to consider her position, she was confirmed in her determination to leave Broomyates. She had seen very little of Scott, and she was sure he was avoiding her, but when that had been impossible, he was as remote as if he scarcely knew her. It was humiliating, and this time, however much Mr. Carlyon hectored her, she wouldn't be persuaded to stay.

But as it happened, Mr. Carlyon took her decision with surprising mildness. He made no effort to persuade her to change her mind, and she realized that at last he had given up all hope of bringing her and Scott together.

"Well, perhaps it would be better for you to go," he said with a sigh. "I don't know what's happened between you and Scott, but it's obvious that I seem to have made a mistake in believing that you and he were right for each other. Perhaps I was wrong about that, and perhaps I'm wrong in thinking that Vanessa won't make him a good wife. I'm getting old and the winters here are too much for me. I think I'll buy that villa in Madeira and settle down there. I've no intention of continuing to live here when Scott marries Vanessa. Whether or not she's an ideal wife for him, she and I will never get on together."

"I know I ought to give you a month's notice, but if you'd let me leave at the end of the week I'd be grateful," said Drina steadily.

"Yes, yes, go when it suits you, and I'll find a temporary secretary."

There seemed no more to say, so she began the task of putting all her notes in meticulous order so that her successor would have no difficulty in finding her way about. Then she broke the news to Elfrida that she would be leaving, and was touched by the older woman's genuine regret.

"Oh, Drina, I am sorry, but I can understand your wanting to be nearer Don."

Now was the time to tell her that the engagement was at an end, but Drina hung back. It wouldn't make any difference to let people believe that she was still engaged to Don, and at the same time it gave her a good excuse for returning to London.

"I hope you haven't let Scott's annoyance upset you. I've told him that you couldn't be held responsible for what happened on Friday night and that ought to be the end of the matter."

"I was very sorry to let you down."

"No harm was done, and if it hadn't been for your encouragement I'd never have tackled the job of organizing the Flower Festival in the first place. It's given me a whole new interest in life, Drina. I'm happier than I've ever been before."

"I'm so very glad," said Drina.

As soon as dinner was over she went across to the stable flat, determined not to stay a moment longer than necessary in Scott's company. Lois was sorting some clothes in the bedroom and called that she wouldn't be long, urging Marc to give Drina a drink.

Drina shook her head. "I don't want one, thank you, Marc. I came over to tell Lois that I'm leaving Broomyates and going back to London at the end of the week. I hope that won't affect your position here."

"There's no reason why it should. Your being here, or not, has nothing to do with my work at the factory, and I intend to stay on. Funny, isn't it, but I want to put down roots here. I never thought I'd hear myself saying that. Freedom from routine always seemed to me the most important thing in life, but I realize now I got my priorities mixed. Unless you're a genius, which I'm not, you need a certain amount of discipline."

"But what about Lois? Does she want to stay on here?"

"No, but she's agreed to give it a year's trial for my sake, and I don't think she'll regret it. I'm looking out for a house or flat in Canterbridge which will make things livelier for her. I prefer the village myself, but Canterbridge is a pleasant little town and I'll be happy to live there."

"I'm relieved to know that I'm not spoiling things for you, Marc. I was afraid that when I left you might consider you ought to go back to London too."

"No, I'm not as altruistic as that," said Marc cheerfully. "By the way, where will you be staying in London? I expect Don's fixed something for you."

"Oh, I shall manage all right," said Drina evasively.

Marc looked at her sharply. "Everything's going ahead between you and Don, isn't it?"

When it came to the point Drina couldn't lie to him, so she said: "No, it isn't. We've broken off the engagement, but I'm not telling people here. It will be simpler to let them believe that I'm going back to London to be near Don."

"But isn't that going to make it very lonely for you, and where will you live? Lois," he said as his wife came into the room, "did you know that Drina had broken off her engagement?"

"Not for certain, but I suspected it," admitted Lois uneasily.

"Then why leave Broomyates?" persisted Marc.

There was nothing for it but to tell him part of the truth.

"Scott and I are not on very good terms, and it makes things rather difficult living in the same house. Don't worry about me, Marc. I'll soon find another job, and somewhere to live, so let's change the subject."

"Of course. Would you two girls like to come down to the village pub for a drink?"

"I'd rather stay here, Marc, thank you," answered Drina, "but you go, and then Lois and I can let our hair down."

"I know when I'm not wanted," he said with a grin, and went out.

Lois grimaced. "He's changed completely. I never thought he'd have settled down to country life so thoroughly; I thought he'd have been bored. As it is, I've had to promise to stay for a year to give the life a fair trial, but as soon as that year's up I'll be on the train to London. You're going next week; you don't know how lucky you are!"

At that something exploded in Drina. All the misery and heartache of the last few days welled up, and she cried passionately: "Lucky, when I'd give anything on earth to be staying on here instead of having to leave! You go sailing on through life, never considering anyone but yourself, and you don't understand the damage you do. That mock engagement...but I can't blame you entirely because if it hadn't been for me you'd never have met Don."

Lois stared at her. "I never thought...I didn't know—"

"Forget it," said Drina wearily. "I'm rather on edge at the moment, or I wouldn't have raved at you like that."

"You're in love with Scott, aren't you? I should have guessed it before this."

"I'm glad you didn't, because I hoped I'd been concealing it successfully."

"And I made you pretend to be engaged to Don and ruined everything."

"No, of course you didn't, and it wasn't fair of me to accuse you of that. Scott's in love with Vanessa; he's never given me a second thought. True, we'd been getting on together much better up to then, but there was no significance in that."

"I'm not so sure," commented Lois. "I've caught him looking at you several times, and I don't believe he's indifferent to you."

"Well, if he wasn't, he is now. You see, I once told him that there was nothing at all except friendship between Don and myself, and then my engagement was announced. I was out with Don when I was supposed to be taking Elfrida to the market, so I acknowledge it's not really surprising that Scott feels he can't trust me."

"But when he knows your engagement to Don is broken off—"

"I shan't tell the Carlyons that it is. It can't make any difference to things as they are, and it's much easier for me if Elfrida thinks that I'm going back to London to be near Don."

"I see," said Lois. "Drina, I'm sorry. I never guessed that my fooling with Don would be so disastrous for you."

"I know you didn't and I never meant to let all this come out. Don't look so upset. I shall go back to London, and find another job, and this time I rather fancy going abroad. I wonder what openings there are?"

Drina talked with determined cheerfulness until Marc came back, and then walked across to Broomyates with her. When he returned, Lois was huddled in a chair, and he said: "Hey, what's the matter? Are you depressed because Drina's going? You've still got me."

"You'd always love me, wouldn't you, Marc?" Lois reached up, and he pulled her out of the chair against him. "Whatever I did?"

"Have you been robbing a bank?" he asked teasingly, "or fiddling the petty cash at the boutique?"

"Neither," she assured him, and his mouth felt for hers and clung.

But all his passionate embraces couldn't stifle her conscience this time. Lois was selfish and pleasure-loving, but she would never have deliberately hurt her sister, and now she was appalled at the consequences of her folly. She told herself that Scott wasn't in love with Drina and never would be, therefore no harm had really been done, and Drina would soon forget him, but she couldn't blot out the memory of her sister's anguished face. Drina wasn't normally emotional, and the fact that she had flared

178

up so violently showed how deep her feelings for Scott were. And just suppose, Lois reasoned, that Drina was mistaken, and that he had no intention of marrying Vanessa but had been beginning to care for her? Then the announcement of her engagement could have jolted him considerably and ruined everything.

The more she thought about it, the more guilty Lois felt. As she lay in bed, with Marc sleeping peacefully beside her, her imagination piled agony on agony until at last she began to sob. Marc, rousing, said sleepily: "Whatever's the matter?" and flinging herself into his arms, Lois wailed: "Even if you never forgive me I've got to tell you what I've done," and poured out the whole tale.

At first he listened in bewilderment, then he pulled himself free of her and sat up, remaining perfectly silent until she had finished. She said fearfully: "I'm sorry, I'm dreadfully sorry. I was frightened when I knew you'd seen Don and me together, and when Vanessa suggested that Don should pretend to be engaged to Drina I agreed because it seemed such an easy way out. I didn't dream that I was doing Drina any harm."

"You only thought of solving your own problem," said Marc grimly. "Are you in love with Don?"

"No, no, and I never was, but I didn't think you'd believe me because of that business in Ibiza. We were only amusing ourselves. He isn't half as attractive as you are, but he was gay, and you've grown so serious since we came back to England."

He looked at her. She could pass for sixteen in the sheer nylon nightdress, her hair hanging to her shoulders. He knew he wasn't blameless. It wasn't her fault that he'd changed so much during the last year while she'd remained the same girl he'd married. He still loved her, even though she couldn't resist basking in the admiration of other men, but Drina mustn't be allowed to suffer for her sister's irresponsibility.

"What are you going to do?" breathed Lois.

"I shall tell Scott Carlyon the truth about that phoney engagement."

"But Drina doesn't want him to know."

"Of course she does, but she couldn't tell him without giving you away, and she wouldn't do that."

"Do you want—will I have to admit to him what I did?"

"No. I'll see him myself, and I shall tell him it was Vanessa's suggestion that Drina should pretend to be engaged to Don. I wonder why she should concern herself in your affairs, why she should want to protect you?"

"Probably because I work for her," pondered Lois.

Marc frowned. "I think there's more to it than that. She isn't the kind of woman to do anything without a very strong motive of self-interest. If she weren't really concerned with helping you, then she must have wanted to embarrass Drina, but why?"

"She's very involved with Scott. Do you suppose she's jealous of Drina?"

"Possibly," said Marc consideringly. "She might not be so confident of marrying Scott as she appears to be, and it could have suited her very well to prevent any deep relationship developing between him and Drina."

"I've just remembered something Drina mentioned. That night she and Don dined at the Country Club, she thought she recognized the man she had seen doing Vanessa's garden hovering about the car park, then she decided she must have been mistaken."

"That's interesting. He certainly wouldn't be dining there, so why should he be hanging about the place? What exactly did Drina tell you about that night? The car ran out of petrol, didn't it?"

"Yes, though Don swore he'd filled it up only that afternoon. He thought his tank must have been leaking, and when he found it wasn't he said that the only other explanation was that someone must have siphoned the petrol out, but for what reason? Nothing could have been gained by doing a thing like that."

"Except a can of petrol, but why pick on Don's car? Of course, the siphoner might have played a trick on more than one person, but I would have thought we'd have heard about it if that had happened. On the other hand, could there have been a particular reason for choosing Don's car? Did someone want it to break down that night?"

"But why?" queried Lois, puzzled. "No one could have been affected by the fact that Drina and Don had to spend the night in the car, apart from Elfrida, because Drina had promised to pick up the flowers for the Festival at the market the next morning. Scott had to go instead, and he was annoyed about that."

"Exactly," said Marc, "and there was another triumph for Vanessa."

"You don't think—?"

"I'm not thinking, only speculating, and I may be quite wrong, but it's possible that this was all part of a plot to discredit Drina in Scott's eyes."

"Then what are you going to do?"

"Leave it to Scott to sort out; it's his affair. I shall tell him what Drina said, what Don said, and he can draw his own conclusions."

"I have a feeling that he cares for Drina."

"Then it's up to him to act. Now settle down and go to sleep."

Lois snuggled up to him. "I've been such a fool, Marc, but I'll never behave so stupidly again. You do forgive me, don't you?"

Marc smiled wryly. "Yes, I forgive you."

She sighed deeply and was asleep in an instant, her troubles forgotten. Marc wondered if it weren't he who was the fool, but knew that he would do the same thing again. She was his wife, and he loved her whatever she did.

At the factory the next morning he asked Scott's secretary if he could be spared for a few minutes. It wasn't an interview Marc relished, but it had to be faced, and he got it over with as quickly as he could. When he had told his tale, Scott surveyed him impassively.

"Thank you," he said. "It couldn't have been easy for you to reveal your wife's part in the affair."

"It wasn't," said Marc frankly, "but I was determined that justice should be done to Drina. Also, there were two points which I wanted to bring to your notice—the fact that Don swore he'd filled up the car that afternoon and that before any of it happened Drina thought she saw Vanessa's gardener in the car park."

"Why should that have any significance?"

"Well, it was Vanessa who urged Lois to persuade Drina to agree to the mock engagement. It seems curious that she should be connected even remotely with the other business."

Scott said: "It could very easily be coincidence, not even that, if Drina were mistaken as she concluded she must be."

"Yes," admitted Marc. He knew the evidence he had offered was flimsy, and he'd gone as far as he was prepared to go. If Scott had any feeling for Drina, he would do some investigating. If he hadn't, then she might as well go back to London and try to forget him.

Scott said: "Can I ask you not to speak of this to anyone else?"

"Certainly," agreed Marc. "My main concern was to put you in the picture."

"I'm grateful to you."

When Marc had gone Scott sat quite still for a moment, and then he rang for his secretary.

"I'm going out," he told her, "and I probably shan't be back until after lunch. If anything crops up it will have to wait."

She stared at him in surprise, even while she murmured: "Very good, Mr. Scott." To her knowledge he had never done such a thing before. What could be the matter?

Scott drove to Broomyates, and parked his car in the drive. Drina, having taken Mr. Carlyon to the factory, was typing busily in the study, and she was astonished when Scott walked in.

"Has anything happened?" she gasped. "Mr. Carlyon?"

"He's perfectly all right. Why didn't you tell me that your engagement to Madderley was only a pretence to shield your sister?"

"How did you—" Drina stopped short. "It wasn't your affair."

"No? Don't you think knowing that would have given me a more tolerant attitude towards your last evening out with him?"

Drina's hurt pride flared up. "It's quite immaterial to me what you think," she lied.

"But it isn't immaterial to me," said Scott curtly. "I dislike misjudging people, and I'm very grateful to your brother-in-law for putting me right."

Drina stared at him. "Marc told you about the engagement? But that means—"

"That his wife has confessed everything."

"I don't understand. Lois was terrified of Marc knowing the truth."

"Apparently her conscience was stronger than her fears, and her husband doesn't seem to have thrown her out, so I assume he's forgiven her. Now, do you really think you saw Vanessa's gardener at the Country Club?"

"I did at the time, but it was only a glimpse, and I don't want to accuse anyone unjustly."

"He's always struck me as rather a shifty character," said Scott thoughtfully. "I think we'll go and have a word with him."

"We?"

"You and I—now."

Scott took her arm, and too bewildered to protest, Drina allowed herself to be led to his car. She couldn't imagine why he was doing all this, but the set of his features didn't encourage questions. He drove to Vanessa's house in the shortest possible time, and without ringing the bell strode up the drive and round to the back of the house. Here there was a wide lawn with rose beds and a greenhouse where, through the glass, Drina could see the gardener stooping over some pots. Scott walked towards it and opened the door unceremoniously.

"I want an explanation," he said without preamble. "Why did you siphon the petrol out of Mr. Madderley's car that night he and Miss Tonbridge were dining at the Country Club?"

Taken completely by surprise, the man turned a sickly grey, then made an attempt at recovery.

"I don't know what you mean," he stuttered, but it wasn't convincing.

"You know exactly what I mean. You were spotted in the car park, and unless you tell me everything I shall get in touch with the police."

Scott's voice was so harsh and his manner so uncompromising that Drina wasn't surprised at the fear in the man's face. He mumbled something about having his orders, and Scott rapped out: "Who gave you those orders?"

"It was Mrs. Mantaressi," the man whined. "She said it was for a joke, and gave me something for my trouble. I never meant to do anybody any harm."

Scott said briefly: "I see," and Drina's heart went out in sympathy to him as they left the greenhouse. It must have been a bitter blow to him to learn that Vanessa was implicated because, clearly, she hadn't meant it as a joke. It was a piece of spite directed against Drina herself.

"Let's leave it at that," said the girl impulsively. "Now that you know the truth, nothing else matters." Then, as she realized what she had said, the colour flooded her face.

"We'll go into that later," answered Scott, "but first, I want a word with Vanessa."

"But she'll be at the boutique."

"Then we'll go there."

Lois was attending to a customer in the shop when Scott strode in, and her eyebrows arched as, after casting a quick glance round to make sure that Vanessa was nowhere in sight, he walked through into the room at the back. Drina would have lingered in the shop, but with a firm grasp on her arm he gave her no chance to stay behind. Vanessa was sitting at a desk adding up some accounts, and she looked up in surprise as they came in.

"Why, Scott," she said, "I didn't expect a visit from you at this time. Is something wrong?"

Her gaze passed to Drina, and for the first time Drina saw a flicker of uncertainty in her eyes.

With brutal directness, Scott demanded: "Why did you bribe your gardener to siphon the petrol out of Don Madderley's car the night he and Drina were dining at the Country Club?"

For a second, Vanessa's teeth dug into her lip, then she recovered herself admirably.

"Really, Scott, you sound just like a policeman," she said lightly. "Your question's too absurd. What motive could I possibly have for doing such a thing?"

"That's what I'm trying to establish."

"My gardener's not very intelligent, you know, and if you rounded on him suddenly and accused him as you did me, then I'm sure he'd admit to anything. I know nothing about Don Madderley's car, and I'm surprised you should think I might."

She faced him with apparent frankness, and Drina was convinced that, no matter what evidence was produced, Vanessa would never admit what she had done. But Scott was ruthless.

"You're lying, Vanessa. When we were children you always lied your way out of awkward situations, and you haven't lost the habit."

Two spots of colour appeared on Vanessa's cheeks.

"Scott, how dare you!" Then her voice softened. "Look, you're under a misapprehension. Let's talk things over calmly by ourselves. Drina, do you mind joining Lois in the shop?"

"Stay where you are, Drina," commanded Scott. "It's no good, Vanessa, you couldn't convince me I'd made a mistake if you talked all night. You owe Drina an apology, and you can make it now."

"You must be mad," said Vanessa incredulously. "Apologize to that mealy-mouthed little hypocrite? Can't you see what she's been about all this time, worming her way into your grandfather's good graces and playing up to you? She didn't want Don Madderley, oh no, because you were a much better catch, and now she's persuaded you that she's an injured party."

"She hasn't persuaded me of anything," said Scott unemotionally, while Drina cried: "I don't want any apology, I don't want to hear anything more about the affair. I'm going back to London!"

She rushed out of the shop and ran towards the Market Square and the Lindisthorpe bus stop, intent on reaching Broomyates and packing her things immediately. She was on the Square before she realized that she hadn't any money with her, and as she stood hesitating, Scott drove up.

"Get in," he ordered, opening the door of the car, but she shook her head.

"No, thank you. I'll make my own way back to Broomyates."

"Without any money? I didn't give you a chance to pick up your handbag before you came out. If you don't get in I shall put you in bodily, which would cause quite a stir. I don't imagine you'd like that."

"You wouldn't dare—" began Drina uncertainly, and then saw by the gleam in his eyes that he meant what he said. She got into the car, and as they drove off, she said childishly: "I hate you!"

Scott made no answer, so she sat there fuming until all at once she became aware that they were heading away from Broomyates.

"Where are you taking me?" she demanded as they sped along a country lane and halted at a grassy clearing which was an entrance to the woods.

"Here," answered Scott. "Hop out."

"I won't," refused Drina, but her words ended in a gasp as he pulled her towards him and his mouth met hers. For a moment she resisted him, and then her bones seemed to melt as she surrendered to an intensity of emotion which ran through her like fire. She was pressed uncomfortably against the handle of the car door, but she never even felt it until Scott lifted his head and said softly: "Do you still hate me?"

Drina began to tremble. If he were playing with her, she couldn't bear it. She'd been certain that he loved Vanessa, and intended to marry her, and now she wasn't sure of anything any more, only that she had betrayed herself completely.

"I want to go back to Broomyates," she said desperately.

"Not yet," answered Scott. "There's no privacy there, so I brought you here to tell you that I loved you. I'm not fooling myself, am I, Drina? You do care for me?"

"More than anything in the world," Drina told him passionately. This time she needn't conceal the leaping flame which enveloped her whole being and gave her a glow which caused Scott's mouth to twist as he caught her to him almost savagely.

"I've been a double-dyed idiot myself. I held off you at first because I thought you were a party to

Grandfather's schemes, and by the time I realized you weren't, it seemed likely that you would marry Madderley."

"I loathed you in the beginning," Drina told him remorsefully, "but though my feelings changed gradually, I was sure you were in love with Vanessa."

"I'll admit that when I met her again the old attraction reasserted itself, but only for a very short time. I was no longer the callow boy who'd been so desperately in love with her; I began to see her for what she was—greedy and egotistical, with no consideration for anyone's welfare but her own. You were so different, but just when I'd begun to appreciate that you announced your engagement to Madderley. I was so furious that I rejected his firm's tender for the community centre. I never wanted to set eyes on him again."

"Then you vented your wrath on me. I was terribly miserable, particularly when you were so insulting after Don and I had been marooned for the night in the car."

"What I said to you then was unforgivable, and my only excuse was that I'd been half out of my mind with worry all night in case you'd had an accident. I know I'm a bad-tempered brute. Do you think you'll be able to put up with me?"

"I'll make a strong effort. Won't your grandfather be triumphant when we break the news to him?"

"I hate to admit this, but he was right all the time. You were the only one for me, only I was too pig-headed to acknowledge it." His arms came round her tightly and he murmured into her hair: "You don't know how wonderful it is to have someone to care. I wasn't very old when my mother left me, and then, when Vanessa deserted me too, I decided that I was better off without women in my life."

They were locked together, and time ceased to have any meaning until all at once Scott exclaimed: "Good lord, I've got an appointment with an important client at two o'clock. I'd completely forgotten about it."

"Then you must be in love," said Drina laughingly. "We'd better drive to the factory right away."

"I'm taking you home first, and then tonight we're going out to dinner together. We've plans to make. I want to marry you as soon as possible."

"But there's a lot to decide first. Where we're to live, for instance."

"At Broomyates, if you're willing. Grandfather really meant it when he talked about buying that villa in Madeira. I think he'd be happy to settle there, and come over to England in the summer to see us."

"And your aunt?"

"Elfrida's never really cared for Broomyates. I know she'd prefer living in a flat in Canterbridge where she could do exactly as she pleased."

"She did once hint as much."

"Then we'll help her find one. Would you be happy at Broomyates?"

"I'd be happy anywhere with you," said Drina simply.

"Don't say things like that when I'm driving and can't stop to kiss you. Do you really mean it?"

"I do."

She sat there in a haze of bliss as the car sped along. It hadn't seemed possible that everything could come right for her, but Scott was here beside her, and it was no dream.

He said: "If you're worrying about Vanessa, I think you'll find that she'll pack up and go back to Rome.

When she does, I was wondering if we couldn't help Lois to take over the boutique. I think she'd make a success of it, and it would give her an incentive to remain here."

"I do believe you're right," said Drina joyfully. "Oh, Scott, it's all too good to be true."

"Not at all," he reminded her. "It's the old fairy tale ending. 'And so they married and lived happily ever after.'"